W9-CPB-655

THE LEGEND
OF
PUNZEL'S POND

Story and Illustrations
by

Judy Hauser

Cherish your Heritage!

Judy

Copyright © 2005 by Judy Hauser

Published by Fen's Rim

PO Box 885, 104 Dexter St.
Elk Rapids, MI 49629
231-264-6800 • www.fensrim.com

All rights reserved. No part of this book may be reproduced
by any means without written permission by the publisher.

First Edition
Printed in the United States of America

Cover Art by Judy Hauser
Book Design by Mark Stone, Fen's Rim

ISBN 0-9713603-0-8

Acknowledgements

The Legend of Punzel's Pond has flowed though my life as a magical river. It began when Grandmother would say, as we walked among the forests of northern Michigan, "Under each of those hills lies a troll." She was born with the gift of a wonderful imagination on October 3, 1890 in Mariestad, Sweden. The hills and waters of Walloon Lake, Little Traverse Bay and Grand Traverse Bay have surrounded my life ever since.

At the headwaters of my magical river was my dear friend, Ruth Ann Carter, who explored the river with me and added zeal to its flow as copy editor. Alice Hanes and Ruth Abrahamson gave the river strength to survive its winding journey. Along its shores were encouraging friends: Mike Sevig of Skandisk, Inc., Gail Hafner, Alexandra Nash, Katie Cunningham and Patty Stearns.

My river flowed as far away as Alaska, thanks to Tim and Anne Stone, and swirled around roots and skimmed sandbars, guided gently by Emma and Hannah Stone. My sons, Kurt and Erik, also wadded through the ripples and eddies to lend support. Above my little river, the beautiful music of Song of the Lakes friends Lisa and Ingemar Johansson curried the currents. Then along came Mark Stone, my publishing guru and cartographer, who waved his divining rod, directed the river's path onto the pages of this book and literally put the Tidendal Valley on the map. Through this journey my husband, Bernd, was by my side walking the forests, meadows and mountains. I believe in the beauty of nature and in the magic and the joy of having wonderful friends.

Fondly,

Judy

Dedicated to my grandparents, Elmer and Judith V., and to my grandchildren, Karli and Kaleb.

The special bond between grandparent and child is truly magical.

JH

Table of Contents

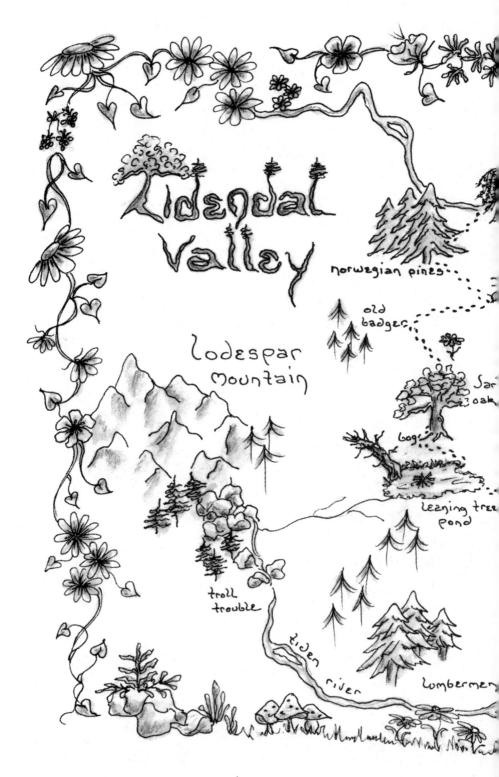

Tidendal Valley

norwegian pines

old badger

Sar oak

bogs

Leaning tree pond

Lodespar Mountain

troll trouble

tiden river

Lumbermen

ravens

tannery

tunnel

tord and lucia's colony

N

W   E

S

cidendal woods

daisy ring

Alf's homestead

to new hope

Foreword

Long ago, when mighty oaks were ladders to the sky and nature frolicked free and wild, Alf, an adventurous young man, was lured deep into the archives of the ancient woods by the sweet scent of pine that permeated the air. He trod beneath the green giants until he came to a break in the vast canopy and discovered a meadow flowing toward distant trees and a mountain beyond.

Anxious to get a better view of the mountain, Alf climbed a near-by oak. Unfortunately this particular tree didn't like intruders and when he was halfway up it started to shake—a shake like a swatter after a fly. The oak accomplished its goal and the young man was sent into a downward spiral. Alf tumbled limb over limb, but fortunately he landed in a patch of friendly daisies.

As Alf adjusted his clothes and apologized to the daisies, he heard soft high-pitched giggles. He followed the happy sounds to a twitching juniper bush. The woodsman parted the branches and discovered a pudgy man, barely two feet tall, nestled against the trunk. The rotund body was shaking with glee. Everything about the fellow was turned up: his pudgy nose, his bushy white mustache, the hems of his coarse earth-colored clothes and the toes of his brown vine-wrapped boots.

Startled by the discovery, Alf could only stare. He had lost his voice.

The fellow's blue eyes twinkled with mirth as they peeked out from under an enormous floppy red hat. His chubby fingers stroked a long white beard while he waited for the tall man to speak.

Finally, curiosity found Alf's voice. "Who are you?" he asked with raspy breath.

Chapter 1
Journey from Sweden

O nce upon a time, in the faraway village of Mariestad, Sweden lived a lively teenage girl named Punzel Nordström and her father Lars. When Punzel was a young child, tragedy struck with the death of her mother. Though Lars Nordström was a loving father, he was also an important businessman and had little time for child rearing. So he left Punzel in the hands of Anna, a kind but over-protective governess. Anna kept Punzel safely behind a fenced yard—but with little chance for playmates. Thus, Punzel spent a lonely childhood. She was soon to graduate from the Finishing School where she'd made a few friends, but she remained shy and longed to be more comfortable with people her own age.

Nevertheless, Punzel had learned to keep a positive attitude and soon she would begin her summer visit with her grandfather, Arne Nordström. Punzel adored her grandfather and appreciated his companionship, as he was a bit shy, too. At Nordvik, her grandfather's farm, she was free to run with the wind and dance in the fields under the long midsummer skies. Besides her beloved Farfar, the farm animals and wild flowers were her favorite companions.

It just so happened that on this particular day, May 12, 1907, Punzel would discover a sudden and unexpected opportunity for change. An official looking letter with black borders was delivered to Nordvik. The message was from an attorney in the United States and stated that Arne's brother, Alf Nordström, had died on his homestead in the distant land of North America. Arne was to inherit his land and legal matters were in urgent need of Arne's attention. A trip was imperative.

Arne, saddened by the news, decided to travel that day to the village of Mariestad, a short distance from Nordvik to tell his youngest son, Lars, about the letter.

"I don't know what to do about this," Arne declared as he handed Lars the letter. "For years Alf begged me to visit him. Now this!" Tears welled up in his sad, weather-lined eyes. "I feel that I have let my bror down. I never felt I could take time away from the farm to make the long journey to America. However, since your mor has passed away and your older bror and his fru have come to live with me, they manage Nordvik as well as I.

"Anders and Ingrid have seen this letter and they told me I should go to America and not worry. I suppose I could be gone and back in a few months. Travel time to America has shortened since Alf left these shores. I can hardly believe that he has been gone from Sweden for thirty-seven years! I wish I could have seen him one more time."

The older, sturdily built man looked down at his well worn leather boots and then back to the concerned look on his son's face. As Arne touched his bushy gray mustache with one forefinger and brushed his fine gray hair back from his furrowed brow, a look of resolve gripped his face.

"Ja, I must go, Lars. This much I can do for him. Tack for listening to an old man's muttering. I will go home and tell Anders and Ingrid my decision."

Punzel was concentrating on her embroidery in the next room but overheard the conversation between her father and grandfather. Suddenly, an idea popped into her head. She put her needle down, flipped her blond braids over her shoulders, as was her habit when she changed thoughts, and began to ponder.

America must be a fine place because Farfar's bror lived there a long time, she said to herself.

I will be graduating from Finishing School this spring. Far wants me to go on with my studies and become a nurse. That I also would like to do, but this might be my chance for the adventure I've been longing for. Perhaps this is my opportunity to become more sure of myself and learn about the new land of America. Far and Anna have decided to marry at Midsommar. They have raised me well, but now I am a young woman. I'm sure Far and Anna would enjoy some time alone after their wedding. I'm old enough to be a lot of help to Farfar on his trip.

Satisfied with this reasoning, her excitement grew as Punzel deftly smoothed her white ruffled pinafore and reached for her scissors. Her blue eyes sparkled as a plan to ask her father's permission started to form.

At the first opportunity, Punzel spoke to her father about her idea. "Far, I happened to overhear Farfar telling you of his decision to go to America. I was thinking . . ." Then, before she lost her courage, she quickly explained why she wanted to go to America with her grandfather.

Lars was very reluctant to give his permission. "Crossing the vast Atlantic Ocean to a strange land where you do not speak the language could be a very dangerous journey, Punzel."

Punzel reminded her father that she was no longer a girl but a young woman. "But Far, I will be seventeen in October. I'll make a terrific companion for Farfar. I am quick to learn. Four hands are better than two. I am good at running errands and can be a big help with the housekeeping while he stays in his bror's cottage. It will only be for a few months. Please Far," she begged. "You won't regret it, and just think of the wonderful education I will get. I'll even have a chance to learn the English language."

Arne also thought the trip would be good for Punzel. They tried very hard to persuade Lars. Reluctantly, Punzel's father finally gave her permission to go. Punzel was filled with pride that she had stuck to her cause and won. But celebration turned to busy preparation as she realized that much had to be done before the day of departure. Steamship tickets had to be purchased and travel papers put in order. Appropriate travel clothing needed to be organized. (It would be cooler on the ocean, and there were many discussions of what items might be needed for their visit to the new land.) Even though it would be summer on both sides of the ocean, a large leather-bound steamer trunk and two leather satchels were required to contain their possessions.

And then, between graduation from Finishing School and preparations for their voyage, Punzel had to spend time at the dressmaker. She was to be the maid of honor at her father's wedding and was to wear a beautiful ankle-length light wool skirt, a white cotton full-sleeved blouse, an embroidered vest and striped apron—a traditional folk costume.

The wedding day was radiant with sunshine beaming on the fresh fields of wildflowers surrounding Nordvik. Early in the day, Punzel and the wedding guests gathered some of the wildflowers for garlands to wear in their hair. Punzel felt like a princess in her new folk dress and enjoyed the company of relatives and her father's and Anna's friends as they ate, sang and danced in celebration. Punzel thought this Midsommar was the best one of all!

Punzel and Arne departed for America two days later. The early morning dew glistened on red tile roofs as a happy but tearful Punzel, sitting in a carriage beside her grandfather, waved farewell to her father, Anna and half a town of well-wishers. She promised to write often and include detailed descriptions of their experiences in the far-away country. Their carriage took them to the port of Göteborg, where they sailed to England. In England they boarded the regal steamship, *H. M. S. Lusitania*, that brought them to the unknown, but beckoning, land of their future.

•   •   •   •   •

When they arrived in New York, their gateway to the new land, Punzel was relieved to learn that her deficiency in the English language was not a problem. At first they had difficulty, but luck traveled with them. They met a Norwegian man who spoke Swedish and English. He helped them find a boarding house with clean, comfortable rooms for their first night in America and gave them directions to the famous Grand Central Station to continue their journey by train the following morning.

Thank goodness for the kindness of that man, she thought.

They had to change trains twice and both times there were problems. At the first change, they almost lost their baggage due to an inattentive porter. During the second change, they misunderstood the train number and nearly ended up on a train going in the opposite direction! The hot, stifling air in the crowded passenger cars gave Punzel a terrible headache made worse by the noisy confusion of people speaking in many languages. After the crisp fresh sea air and relatively smooth Atlantic crossing by ship, the train ride was tiring and made for a disappointing introduction to America.

As Punzel and Arne arrived at the end of their rail journey in the village of New hope, an empty passenger car, serving as a depot, was their only greeting.

Quite a difference from our departure in Sweden, Punzel thought.

Since there was no railroad attendant on duty they decided to leave their satchels and trunk on the narrow train platform and walk toward the cluster of wooden buildings that made up the village.

Punzel stepped gingerly around the tree stumps that dotted New Hope's main street. "Stumps in the middle of a road!" she laughed. Her long strides kicked up a fine film of dust that clung to the hem of her dress, lace petticoat and dainty high-buttoned shoes. *Now, this isn't so funny*, she thought in dismay. Soon they came to a series of rough-sawn plank walkways that made a makeshift sidewalk by the store fronts. Though the boards were a welcome respite from walking on the soft dusty ground, Punzel still had to watch her step lest she lose her footing on the uneven boards.

They found Karl Lundquist's office, Alf's attorney, however he had been called out of town.

Then, another disappointment. New Hope didn't have a livery. With no place to hire a horse or buggy, Arne and Punzel asked several people if they knew of someone who might help them with transportation to the Alf Nordström homestead. Many of the village people spoke Swedish and fondly remembered Alf, but they didn't know anyone who had a spare horse or conveyance of any kind.

New Hope had one general store and in its window hung a sign announcing "Fresh Cheese." Punzel's rumbling stomach reminded her that the small sandwiches served on the train weren't going to satisfy her appetite for much longer. She turned expectantly to her grandfather.

"Perhaps the store's proprietor can help us find transportation and we can buy something to eat," Punzel suggested.

Then she grabbed her grandfather's arm and almost pulled him through the front door.

Gracious, she thought. *I haven't been in this country very long and already I'm getting more determined, or is it that I'm really hungry.*

After their dusty walk they were surprised to see the store's spotlessly waxed wooden counters. Their weary spirits revived with the tantalizing smell of freshly baked bread and they were delighted to find milk, eggs, butter and that wonderful smelling homemade bread for sale next to large wheels of the advertised cheese. Mr. Nelson, the proprietor, was very welcoming and glad to help them with supplies, but he was sorry that he couldn't give them help regarding transportation to Alf's homestead. While Arne paid for their groceries, a tall slender young man approached the counter. He spoke in Swedish and introduced himself as Gus Larsson. Punzel noticed he had brought a new shovel and an ax to the counter.

"I heard you ask about hiring a rig. We do not have spare horses in this area. Every animal is needed to work the soil and haul logs. I live on my parents' farm two miles to the north, past Mr. Nordström's property. I will be glad to take you and your baggage there after I make my purchases. I was very sorry to hear of Alf's passing. He was a fine man and a good friend. He did much to help my parents and I would welcome the opportunity to return a favor to any relative of his."

Arne gratefully accepted the young man's offer. They each carried an armful of parcels out to the waiting wagon. Gus helped Punzel climb onto the high wagon seat where she perched between the two men as they rode to the train station to pick up the Nordströms' trunk and satchels.

Sweden seems more civilized, she thought, as they bumped along over the ruts, stumps and loose sand on the narrow road running north from the village. Where the road ran through a swampy area, logs had been laid like corduroy fabric across it to keep the wagon wheels from getting stuck in the soft ground. The springs on the high seat squeaked with each jolt as the huge wheels lurched, rolled and slid over the slick logs. Their slow travel gave Punzel time to observe the forests they passed through while she acclimated herself to the wagon's motion. Surprisingly, she saw that many trees were the same as those in Sweden—oak, pine, birch and beech. Even the crops of wheat, oats, potatoes and beans growing on the cleared farmlands between the forests were familiar. *This country is not so strange after all*, she concluded.

Gus certainly is kind, Punzel continued to muse. When they arrived at Alf's homestead, he unloaded their baggage and purchases from the wagon and helped Arne carry the heavy trunk into the cottage. After they thanked him, he promised he would stop by soon to see if they needed more supplies.

Gus is not only kind but good looking too, with the warmest brown eyes, and much taller than me, she observed as his wagon continue down the road. *Maybe we could become friends if I could get over my bashfulness.* Meanwhile, she couldn't help smiling as she thought of his last name. It meant Lar's son. There had been a Lars in his family also.

Arne broke into her thoughts. "Punzel, you sure do like to daydream. Are you admiring the flowers over yonder or are you thinking about the young man who brought us here?" He had seen the smile on Punzel's face and now the sudden blush on her cheeks gave him his answer. Her grandfathers words drew her attention to the masses of flowers and herbs in the nearby fields.

"Farfar, look! There is a beautiful heart-shaped pond behind Alf's cottage!" Punzel, her flaxen-hair flying, dashed across a fragrant carpet of thyme, tiptoed through a wild strawberry bed, leaped over patches of pink and blue cornflowers, and finally came to rest upon a weathered, vine-laden bridge spanning the pond's shores. Her hunger was momentarily forgotten as she looked back at her companion and waited for him to join her.

Arne, Punzel's travel-weary grandfather, slowly made his way toward her, and as he approached the pond's clear waters, she saw his face brighten and his steps gain in vigor. Arne paused by a thicket of berry bushes beside the foot of the bridge.

"My bror's homestead looks just like his letters described." He sighed and looked beyond the pond to the forest's majestic old trees. "It has been a long, difficult trip, but I'm glad we came."

"I never dreamed that our journey would bring us to such an enchanting place, Farfar." Punzel stooped to pick a small bouquet of daisies growing at the waters edge. "These flowers, your bror Alf's little cottage, and the old forest remind me of home and your farm, but this heart-shaped pond looks truly magical!"

"Ja," her grandfather agreed as he studied the unusual purple berries growing in the bushes before him. "There must be magic here to grow such fruit as this. Look at the size of these berries! Each one is bigger than my thumb nail!" They eagerly sampled a few berries and promised that they would be back to pick more.

"Now," Arne insisted as he popped the last juicy berry into his mouth, "we need to get settled in Alf's cottage. I looked over the inside when Gus and I brought the trunk in and it is amazingly free of dust. The air must be special, too," he teased.

"I'm right behind you," Punzel replied thinking that she would be back soon to explore the area around the beautiful heart-shaped pond.

Alf's rustic cottage was in good condition, both inside and out. Punzel was surprised at how cozy the inside was as she admired the stone fireplace that rose into a loft and out through the roof. Between a large cast iron stove and the sink, a black pitcher pump stood highlighted by the sun's rays peeking through the cheery kitchen window. *Oh, good*, she thought, *at least we don't have to carry water from the pond.*

On the bare oak floor stood a wooden trestle table with a pine tree carved in each end leg. Two benches adorned with smaller carved pine trees rested on either side. The back door was flanked by a wall cupboard on the right and a linen cupboard on the left. The wall cupboard was filled with a large variety of carved bowls, plates and utensils. Across the room a single stool crowded a small table laden with knives and partially carved wooden pieces. Nearby, pegs hung clothing as though buttoned to the knotty pine wall. One peg held a leather carving apron.

As if to oversee the carving process, a tall narrow bookcase stood at the ready to offer advice. "Alf must have liked to read", observed Punzel, admiring the shelves containing books of all sizes and shapes. *I will spend a lot of time looking as these*, she promised herself.

In the far corner rested a handsome, intricately carved closet bed. A carved moose standing at the edge of a pond adorned with water lilies crowned the top. Its supporting posts were entwined with the heart-shaped leaves of the moonflower vine. The bed's side panels depicted small woodland animals: rabbits, otters, field mice, and the like. Two front doors opened to reveal a bed with a down mattress. A large cut-out heart surrounded by carved lingonberries was centered in each door. "Oh, Farfar, what a fanciful bed!"

"Ja, I can see that Alf became a master at woodcarving." Arne remembered his brother always with a knife and piece of wood in hand. "Many times he got bawled out by our Far when he was caught whittling instead of watching the cows in the pasture. He preferred working with wood to farming. The family thought that he should have paid more attention to farming, but now I see carving was his real joy. I think that is why he wanted to leave home and find a place where he could do what he wanted."

"I like this cottage, Farfar. I could make it into a real home for us. I can braid rugs and make curtains for the windows. I'm a pretty good cook, too. I learned a lot at Finishing School."

Her grandfather tried to hide a smile. "Whoa, little one. You are going too fast for me. You remind me of a galloping young pony. We came here to take care of Alf's affairs, not to make a new home for ourselves. We must take each day one at a time. First let us eat. You must be as hungry as I am."

"I'm glad we bought the fresh food in the village. Those few berries did little to satisfy my hunger. I'm starved!" Punzel quickly set the trestle table with a couple of plates, cups and utensils she selected from the cupboard. "This is like our very first picnic, Farfar."

After their meal they were anxious to examine the many bowls, cups, spoons, and knives in the cupboard. Each piece had exquisitely carved details, some with woodland flowers, others sporting leafy vines or wild fruit and berries. An immediate favorite of Punzel's was a rather large bowl with a swooping bird on the side. Even the utensils had ornate designs on the handles. There were many spreader knives, used for spreading butter, jams and soft cheese. These were smaller than regular knives and their blades were carved into the same wood as the handles. Punzel remembered her grandmother was especially fond of using this kind of knife.

The spoons came in all sizes and shapes too, but one spoon stood out. The end of its handle was shaped into an elf's head wearing a tall hat. *Now, why would a tomte be carved onto a spoon?* Punzel wondered. She had seen pictures of elves in storybooks, but on a spoon?

After admiring the cupboard's treasures, Arne declared that they needed to find a cool place to store their perishable dairy products. "Punzel, it seems that I get sidetracked as easily as you. It must be a family trait," he chuckled. To complete this task, they decided to investigate the area by the waters of the heart-shaped pond. From the back door, a short path led them to a bubbly spring of cold water where a wooden box had been built over its flow.

"This spring must feed the pond," Arne noticed as he watched the water disappear beneath the box and reappear in the direction of the pond. He opened the clasp on the side of the box, lifted the heavily hinged lid and felt the enclosed, cool, damp air escape. Along the sides of the box they saw rock ledges. "And this must be where Alf kept his milk and butter from spoiling." Smiles of satisfaction spread over their faces.

They also needed to secure light for the late evening and early morning hours. (In those days, electricity was only the dream of a promise to come for country folk.) "The sun doesn't seem to stay in the sky as long as it did in Sweden," observed Punzel.

"Ja, we have many new ways to get used to." Arne was already at the task of locating oil for the lamps. They found the oil under the kitchen sink. There were three oil lamps in the main room, one hung over the sink and one stood on each table. There were also two oil lanterns hanging on iron hooks—one at the front door and one at the rear door—that looked like they were used to guide night and early morning visits to the out house and the large shed beyond.

While Arne checked the oil level in the lamps, Punzel thought about where she would sleep. As Arne was a tall, rather portly man, she decided that he should sleep in Alf's bed.

"It's only right for you to have your bror's bed, Farfar. I would like to use the loft, if I may. It would be fun to sleep up there—like having a room to myself. The ladder at the end of your bed is just my size." She didn't wait for his answer as her slender body was already climbing to the loft. At the top she found a small, filled oil lantern, which she quickly lit.

The room above was as simple as the room below. A railing with cut-out pine trees guarded the loft's edge. Her lantern cast friendly shadows on the ceiling and illuminated a huge, wooden steamer trunk hugging the wall in front of her.

It's cozy under the peak of the roof. I might get some warmth from the chimney in winter, she mused. *Oh,* she caught herself, *here I go again thinking I can convince Farfar to let us stay.*

Punzel couldn't resist opening the trunk and was rewarded by finding several blankets and a down comforter. *I'm glad I looked in there,* she congratulated herself.

"Farfar, I just found an old trunk with extra bedclothes!" she called down. "I'm going to fix a place for myself to sleep and then I'll prepare dinner." As she finished her task, she noticed small furniture made visible in the waning daylight by a tiny window cut into the end wall next to the chimney. She carried her lantern closer for a better look. A small chair carved out of a solid log, a miniature trestle table, a small posted bed, and a dainty bedside table sprang to life under her lantern's glow. *This end of the loft looks like living quarters for a small child,* she thought. *Why would Alf have such furniture,* she puzzled, *and what purpose would a tiny window like that serve?*

The lantern's light also revealed a shelf niche in the chimney's stones. The shelf contained several books of normal size. She was a curious girl and didn't see any harm in looking at them. An old book with wooden covers caught her attention. She reached for the book, noticing the soft patina that wood gets after much use. She ran her fingers over the upper cover and their touch revealed a relief carving of an elf surrounded by a heart of lingonberries. Another tomte! Her hands shook with excitement as she carefully turned back its cover.

Chapter 2
The Journal

As Punzel opened the wood-covered book, the words, "Tidskrift av Alf Nordström" leaped before her eyes. Oh, this is Alf's journal! I shouldn't read this without Farfar's permission. I'd better show it to him right away. Punzel got up from her seat by the stone chimney and quickly descended the loft's ladder.

Arne was sitting on the stool by the small table examining the unfinished carvings of his brother. "Farfar, Alf kept a diary. I have found Alf's journal!" An excited Punzel handed Arne the wood-covered book. "Look! The cover has the same tomte carved into it as the spreader knife." The old man's eyes lit up in astonishment. He motioned Punzel to sit beside him and together they started to read.

"1 Juni, 1870. I must put my thoughts onto paper. I have a feeling that this United States of America is the right place for me. Today I visit an incredible piece of property. Such beauty. There's a charming heart-shaped pond, surrounded by berry bushes and wild peppermint. Wild apple trees dot the landscape and in the forest grow hard woods of oak, ash, beech, birch. Magnificent Norwegian Pines lead my eye to a mountain beyond.

"15 Juni, 1870. I explore the lower woodland and discover mushrooms, edible ferns, and wild onions. I'll not starve here. Already I begin to feel at home and it has only been two weeks since my arrival. I'm tired from walking and climbing, but the daylight is long and I have much to do. Thankfully I find shelter with my friend, John Johnsson. His mother is visiting a sister in Chicago. I sleep temporarily in her room. John was right to persuade me to come here. His farm lies to the north of this land. Farms are much larger than in Sweden. Nearby families speak Swedish also. I feel already at home! I've decided to accept the homestead plan. I will be given this 160 acres FREE if I stay and improve the land during the next five years. I have to be twenty-one to make the file official, but that will happen soon! The United States has good idea!

"3 Juli, 1870. A bubbling spring feeds the heart-shaped pond. It has good taste. Refreshing to drink on these hot summer days. I'm building my cottage close to this spring.

"8 Augusti, 1870. There's little time to write as I've managed to plant a small garden while I build a cottage. The soil is good, my plants doing well. I'm grateful for the kindness of neighbors. They have much to do in their fields, yet they find time to help me. The gathering of rocks and small stones for the foundation, fireplace and chimney was hard work, but I'm rewarded with good, strong walls. I work from first light of day till dark of night when my lantern burns out of oil.

"30 September, 1870. Chimney is finished! Roof is finished! I even install windows! I never knew I would use so much wood on my small cottage, but the walls are as tight as I can make them. Sarah Andersson, John's girlfriend, has kept up my strength with her home baked pies and cookies. They have had sadness. John's mother passed away in Chicago on Sept. 5. John told me she was determined I come to America to get this property. I never knew I made such an impression on her when we were neighbors in Sweden. I remember she liked my wood carvings. I'm sorry I didn't get chance to see her in this country. John and Sarah had planned on wedding at Christmas. I'm not sure that will happen now, with their sadness.

"14 Oktober, 1870. I live in my cottage! My fireplace has proven worthy. The cold and dampness remain outside, the warmth from my fires make little cottage cozy. I need to chop more firewood this week, then I build bed to sleep on. I cannot sleep on floor in nest of pine boughs throughout the winter. I made small table and stool when the weather was too wet for outside work. Bed will be made in same weather this fall.

"5 November, 1870. Potatoes, beets, carrots, onions and small squash from my little garden are stored in little cellar I dug under the back of the cottage. I feel good about what I have accomplished. Bed is finished except I think for carving some pictures on it. That

12

will take a year of rainy days. At last I'm sleeping above floor.

"22 December, 1870. My twenty first birthday! Today I celebrate! My file at land office to homestead is official! How good it feels. A real birthday surprise! Sarah and John brought me down filled mattress for new bed. I got rid of pine boughs fast!

"13 Januari, 1871. Celebration! John and Sarah decided to get married at Christmas after all. They felt his mother would have wanted it that way. It was nice occasion, but I miss my family. The forest abounds with animals. I must carve some on bed!

"4 Februari, 1871. Much snow on ground, but spring still flows. I don't see many animals or tracks now. If more snow, it will reach the front windows.

"24 Mars, 1871. I'm glad I put aside dry wood to make extra ax handles and other useful tools. Is long winter in this country too.

"27 April, 1871. Snow finally gone and ice off heart-shaped pond. I like to celebrate Swedish spring. I gather up fallen branches and dried vines from little garden and build bonfire. Is good custom to clean up debris from last year and welcome spring with clean yard.

"4 Mai, 1871. Wrote to Arne again. I want him to come see what I have accomplished in America. I think he sure I not stay through winter. I hardly believe I been here almost one year."

This entry brought mist to Arne's eyes.

"Punzel, I believe we should stop reading now and continue again tomorrow. I grow a little sad in remembering, but I think this journal was written with the hope that one day I would read it and understand his life in the new land. It is good that we have come. Let us have a simple dinner, child. I'm not very hungry. It has been a very eventful day."

They ate their soup in companionable silence as each was thinking of the revelations of Alf's journal.

"God natt, Farfar," Punzel called as she climbed the ladder to the loft and stretched out on the soft comforter, glad she didn't have to sleep on pine boughs. Only then did she remember the little furniture by the chimney. *I was so excited after finding Alf's journal that I forgot to tell Farfar. I must tell him in the morning*, she promised herself.

Breakfast, was an exercise in concentration as Punzel got acquainted with the huge cast iron stove. It was difficult getting the heat just right to fry eggs over a wood fire. Thoughts of the little furniture in the loft were once again pushed to the back of her mind.

They had barely finished eating when there was a knock at the front door. "Who could that be?" Arne eyebrows went up as he looked at his granddaughter. "News of our arrival travels fast!"

Punzel went to the door and greeted the stranger. He looked to be about her grandfather's age. Under his wide-brimmed straw hat, he wore a hand-woven shirt tucked into baggy tan pants. "God dag," he greeted her in Swedish. "I am your neighbor, John Johnsson." He turned toward Arne. "A lot of years have passed since we were growing up in Sweden. I heard from Gus Larsson that you had arrived. Välkommen to the Tidendal Woods. That is what we call Alf's homestead. I'm sorry for your loss. Alf, as you know, was my best friend. I have brought over Stig and Gotta, Alf's horse and goat. They have been in my care since his passing. It was the least I could do. Now I think you can make use of them."

"Tack for your kindness." Arne rose to shake hands with their visitor. "A lot of years have passed on both sides of the water. This is my barnbarn, Punzel.

"I know you persuaded Alf to come to this land. You did right! Alf has made a nice home. But our time here is short. We came only to see Alf's attorney and settle the property's ownership."

"It's a shame you won't be staying," replied Farmer Johnsson. "It's sad to see this place without family. Such a pretty spot and a very special one."

"Ja, I agree," Arne nodded his head. "But I still have a good farm in Sweden and Punzel must get back to her schooling. She plans on becoming a nurse."

"I hope you change your mind. It would be nice to have you living here. Keep the animals for now. There is a wagon in the shed. Stig is happy pulling it. He should give you ample transportation to the village and back. Bales of clean straw for bedding are stored in one corner of the shed and plenty of hay, oats and grain have been left in the barrels. I had a feeling you would come. Gus can stop by my farm and bring over more feed as you need it. Sarah wants to invite you both to dinner after you settle in. We are anxious to hear about your trip and catch up on news of our friends in the old country. The letters from home come slowly and not as often as we would like."

He turned to leave, but looked back as he stepped out the door.

"I believe that Alf's land has special powers. It just might work its magic on you." With a wink and a parting wave of his hand, Farmer Johnsson left.

"Farfar, what a kind man! Now we can get our own fresh milk from Gotta, and Stig will give us transportation to New Hope." Then Punzel got a puzzled look on her face. "I wonder what he meant by 'Alf's land has special powers.'"

"John was just teasing us. He was full of fun when he was young also," her grandfather smiled. "I think Alf's attorney might be in his office today. I need to take care of our business as soon as possible. Would you like to come with me and pick up flour and whatever else we need? I'll check on the animals' feed, put Gotta in the pasture and hitch Stig to the wagon Mr. Johnson talked about. I'm sure it's in good condition like everything else around here."

"I would love to go, Farfar. Besides the supplies, may I pick out some cheerful fabric to make curtains? Maybe there will be enough left over to start a quilt for my bed."

"Punzel," Arne chuckled, "once you get an idea, you never give up on it."

Their afternoon in New Hope was a great success. Mr. Lundquist was back from his trip to Chicago and apologized for not being in town when they arrived. Then he gave Arne papers to read and said he would come out to Alf's cottage at the end of August, giving Arne time to decide the destiny of Alf's land. He, too, was hoping Arne would stay in America—after all, this was the wonderful land of opportunity! At the general store Mr. Nelson packed their supplies and helped Punzel find fabric for her curtains and pieces for a bed quilt. She was determined to show her grandfather how nice she could make their American home.

The days flew by. August would soon be upon them. Arne admired how the new curtains cheered up the inside of Alf's little cottage and decided it wouldn't hurt to make a few changes on the outside. He painted the walls red and the trim white in the traditional Swedish cottage colors. Next he made shutters with a cut-out heart in the center for the two front windows. Then he painted the shutters and the front door blue, the color of the forget-me-not, Punzel's favorite flower. Punzel loved the new look, but asked why he was working so hard if they were not going to live there?

"I'm trying to make it easier to sell," Arne replied. "People admire a well-kept home so I thought I would fix it the way we like."

While Arne painted, Punzel decided to identify the plants around
the cottage and the pond. She recognized many varieties that also
grew in the forest near Nordvik, including the tart red lingonberries,
similar to small cranberries, and the pink, bell-shaped flower, linnea,
also called twin flower, because there are two flowers on each stem.
She found these intermingled with the berry bushes. And the vigor-
ous peppermints were crowding the flowers. *I suspect Arne spent a
lot more time carving than working in his gardens,* Punzel chuckled.
Perhaps dividing these plants into
separate areas would make it easier to
manage.

Dinnertime was spent talking about
their day's adventures and afterward
reading from the journal if they
weren't too tired. It was a pleasant
time for Punzel and her grandfather.
They developed a camaraderie that had not
been possible in previous years. They used the time to explore one
another's interests. Grandfather would talk about his walks in the
wonderful woods of the Tidendal valley. Punzel would share her garden discoveries. Time and beauty were allowing them to build the
special bond that can form between grandparent and grandchild.

Punzel fell asleep as soon as her head touched the pillow and
dressed hurriedly each morning, anxious to begin the new day. There
was no more thought given to the little furniture by the chimney.

•　　•　　•　　•　　•

Mr. Lundquist arrived the last week of August. Punzel was worried that there hadn't been enough reasons or time for Arne to
change his mind. She didn't know that the land had grown fond of
her and her grandfather and was busy working its magic. She didn't
hear the wind swirl softly whispering, "Stay, stay, stay." She didn't
see the flower heads nod in agreement, nor did she notice the trees
full of woodland birds singing "this is your home now."

"The old homestead looks great." Mr. Lundquist said while he
surveyed the freshly painted building and its surroundings. You have
made a lot of improvements. Does this mean you have changed your
mind about leaving, Mr. Nordström?"

Arne cleared this throat, paused and glanced at Punzel. "It has
been a special time living on this wonderful land with my barnbarn.
There is no easy way to know what is best. Perhaps it would be pos-

16

sible to assume ownership of Alf's land for one year? Then we will be able to see more of the future. I know Punzel wants to stay longer and how can I deny her the opportunity?"

Arne turned to Punzel. "I see that living here a while longer would be the experience of a lifetime for us. So, I wrote to your far and his bror and told them we would like to stay for a year. They both agreed we should stay. Ja, Punzel," he continued, seeing the surprised look on her face, "I have grown to love this land as much as you do. I could not say anything until I had your far's and far-bror's blessings."

"Well, I certainly think your request is reasonable." Mr. Lundquist smiled and handed a paper to Arne. "I'll turn ownership of the land over to you. Please sign on the bottom of this paper." With a flick of the pen, their future was decided, at least for another year. Tears clouded Punzel's blue eyes as she hugged and thanked her grandfather.

The next day Punzel worked with renewed energy. "We can stay for a year," she hummed over and over. And as she hummed a new plan for her gardens formed. She would divide the land around the pond into seven heart-shaped gardens: one for herbs, one for edible flowers, one for strawberries, one for lingonberries, one for raspberries, one for vegetables, and one for pretty flowers. *There will be lots of hearts on our land,* she noted with satisfaction. *The "our" sounded good, too.*

She decided the rough-hewn bridge across the pond was the perfect place to contemplate the location of each garden. Her fingers touched the heart-shaped leaves of the moon flower vines as she sat on the bridge. Their tendrils appeared to caress the coarse wood and the beautiful white, trumpet-shaped blossoms seemed to sway in time to the wind's music. *These are the most prolific vines I have ever seen,* thought Punzel. *Their foliage is so dense it's as though they're trying to hide something.* She laughed at such a silly thought.

She crossed to the pond's far bank and found clusters of large, purple berries on thickly entwined bushes. She tasted the fruit and savored their sweet, nutty flavor. *These look like cousins to the berries Farfar saw when we first arrived. I shall bake them into a pie for a surprise.*

Across the pond, Punzel's eyes caught the vibrant red of a water lily blossom. *I have never seen a red lily before. I must look in Alf's journal and see if he mentioned one. There are many wonderful*

17

plants on his Tidendal Woods homestead.

Beyond the floating garden of lily pads Punzel spotted an island. Tall grass and cattails grew around the small spot of land. *That looks like an inviting place for birds to nest in the spring.* "The spring! I will be here in the spring," she sang as she continued her exploration.

Punzel passed many large rocks, tree stumps and hollow logs along the shore and finally stopped for a drink by the bubbling spring that fed the pond. *This water tastes like the water from our pitcher pump. How clever of Alf to bring this wonderful water into the cottage.*

As often as time would allow, Punzel and Arne would read Alf's journal. They learned of the great Chicago fire and the completion of the transcontinental railroad in 1871. They got a lesson in American history as well as a record of Alf's life. They found a mention of the red water lily. Alf remembered seeing similar lilies in a Swedish park. The likeness between their home in Sweden and Alf's home in America was truly amazing.

The journal taught Punzel about the various plants and how to care for them. Her designs for the garden became more intricate as she was stimulated by Alf's written words. She gathered those ideas and sketched them to show her grandfather.

"You've taken on a lot of work for yourself," he remarked. "You really need a helper. I'll try to give you a hand when I've finished the project I'm working on."

"What are you working on?" asked Punzel.

"It's a surprise," came the answer. "No more questions."

Punzel observed that her grandfather had a definite mysterious air about him. Little did Punzel and Arne know that unseen ears listened carefully to their conversation.

Chapter 3
A Secret Revealed

Punzel's daytime activities became routine—eat breakfast, look over the garden plans sketched the previous evening, don an outdoor pinafore and work in the gardens till noon. Sew after lunch when she could make use of the best daylight to see her tiny stitches. Then back to the gardens as the heat of the day subsided. There wasn't much time for day dreaming. Every minute had to be put to good use in the last days of summer.

It was then that competition between Punzel and the honey bees increased. While she dug and relocated plants, they gathered nectar in the nearby flowers, each trying to keep out of the other's way. She often whispered to her tiny winged companions, "You are such hard workers. Farfar's bror left us many jars of your delicious, sweet honey. We eat it every day. Thank you!"

"Buzzzzzzzz," they replied, guarding their secret.

Each morning as the gardens progressed, Punzel would make a quick survey of the previous day's accomplishments. What she saw gave her encouragement and pride. But during one search, Punzel noticed a portion of her planned work for the day had already been done. What a puzzlement! She rubbed her eyes in wonder. Overcome with curiosity, she decided to start the next day with a peek at the gardens BEFORE breakfast. She could hardly wait for the next morning.

Yes, indeed! The dawn light revealed more work had taken place during the night. Something strange was happening in her gardens. The only logical explanation was that her grandfather had been trying to surprise her.

"You don't think I have enough work to do?" he joked when Punzel told him of her suspicions. "Ha! Your unseen worker wasn't me. Perhaps you've found yourself a tomte."

"Farfar, you're making fun of me! You know tomtar only exist in folk tales." Nevertheless, Punzel kept looking for further evidence of good deeds. She got an answer in a rather overwhelming way.

Gotta, the goat, was very nosy. She often observed Punzel gathering greens and flowers from the gardens. *If they're good for Punzel, then they're good for me,* Gotta thought. Looking was not enough for the head-strong goat. She needed to satisfy her curious appetite. That morning she found a weak board in her pasture fence, squeezed through, and headed straight for the nearest garden.

Punzel, intent on transplanting strawberries, didn't notice Gotta enjoying the tender new leaves of the fall lettuce in the next garden until she heard a "Burp! Burp!"

What was that? The startled gardener glanced toward the source of the sound.

"Gotta! What are you doing in my garden? Get back in your pasture," Punzel demanded.

Gotta had not had her fill of the tasty greens and remained where she was, contentedly chewing. Punzel, agitated at being ignored, ran after the offensive goat, waving her hands in desperation. Gotta thought it a game and ran through each garden, pausing for a quick taste as if she was happily saying, "Never let a good opportunity pass you by." Punzel pursued the frolicking goat from bean to berry, chamomile to chive, each of them leaving a path of trampled plants in their wake.

At last, Punzel was able to catch Gotta, whose greed got the best of her as she paused too long over some luscious blackberries. The delinquent goat was led back to the pasture in disgrace as Punzel admonished her for such bad behavior. "You should stick to eating acorns and grass and leave my plants alone!"

Walking back to her ruined gardens, Punzel looked on in despair. *How am I going to straighten up that mess?* All energy spent, she decided to wash her hands and start dinner. *Tomorrow is another day, as Farfar would say,* she thought and wiped a tear from her cheek. *Perhaps it won't look so bad in the morning.*

As she approached her gardens the next morning, an amazing sight greeted her. The trampled plants had been righted. She couldn't

20

believe her eyes. *This is either magic or someone is tricking me. These plants couldn't have straightened up by themselves,* she reasoned. *Someone must be tricking me.* Bending to get a closer look at each plant, she saw strange impressions in the dirt. *Why, they look like shoe prints, but they couldn't be Farfar's. These are smaller than mine.* Determined not to mention this discovery lest she be teased, she devised a plan to solve the mystery herself.

After an early bedtime, she awoke before dawn, put on her work pinafore, and tip-toed out of the cottage. The early morning mist muted the landscape and draped the pond and gardens in a mystical veil. Punzel wished she had thought to wear a shawl as she shivered in the cool damp air. No sooner had she found a comfortable position behind an outcropping of rocks when she heard a soft sing-song voice drift through the murky still air.

"I am a little tomte, as good as I can be, I'll dig and plant 'til dawn has come and no one knows it's me!"

Peering between the rocks, Punzel saw the shimmer of a small lantern's light. Enveloped in its glow was a short pudgy man underneath a tall red hat. On his feet were open-heeled shoes that turned upward at the toes. His socks and sleeves were striped in red and white. A dark gray coverall was barely visible beneath his long bushy white beard. He was busily thinning a row of lettuce, believing that he was quite alone.

Punzel's eyes blinked in disbelief! *Am I awake or still in bed dreaming? I have to be brave. I must find out who that little man is.* Silently, she left her hiding place and crept toward the lantern. In a few moments, she was beside the little figure and reached down to touch his shoulder.

"Uh, excuse me, sir." The little man jumped as she spoke, causing her to jump also.

"Oh, I'm sorry! I didn't mean to startle you," she continued, "but I had to see if you were really real!"

Regaining his composure, the little fellow bent to brush dirt of his knees and pick up his fallen shovel. "Of course I'm real! I'm a REAL elf. I'm Pung, Alf's tomte, at your service."

"I'm pleased to make your acquaintance. My name is Punzel."

The little fellow sighed and looked up at the lovely young woman. "I knew it was only a matter of time before you found me out, but I liked your idea about the heart-shaped gardens and I thought I could help. I do like to be useful. Well, what's done is done and probably for the best. It's the honey that really gave me away."

"Honey, what honey?" Punzel sat down to be at the little man's level.

"You ate the honey that Alf got from the bees who gathered the nectar from the magical daisies. That's how you can see me or any other magical creature," Pung explained. "If daisies grow in a fairy ring, they produce magical pollen and the bees convert it into magical nectar. We tomtar can only be seen by a human if the human steps into a daisy ring or eats the honey made from the daisy nectar.

"Alf fell into a daisy ring long ago, inhaled the daisy pollen, and later ate the honey. Ha, ha, ha—a double whammy! Magical daisy rings are VERY rare, so what were the chances? After I was visible to Alf we became friends and have shared many adventures. He also taught me how to carve. I'm pretty good at it too.

"When you and Arne arrived, I hid Alf's journal in my book shelf because I wasn't sure what you were like. That book should only be read by humans who care as much about this place as he did. Alf talked a lot about his bror, but he didn't know you since were born many years after we came to this country. I'm glad Arne has decided to stay for a year. That means I can stay too. Otherwise it would have been my obligation to go back to Sweden as your farfar's tomte. I've been really lonely since Alf died, but I've come to like this place and was not ready to leave."

"You came with Alf?" Punzel was trying to remember all that she had heard.

"I sure did. Wherever Alf went, I went. Although we didn't go to any far away places until we made the big ocean trip. I've had a wonderful life here, especially after he was able to see me. If we had stayed in Sweden, he probably would never have known that I exist. The Tidendal Woods is a magical land where wondrous powers abide. Perhaps you will understand one day!"

"Hummm. You are the second person to tell me that." Punzel flung back her braids still trying to collect her thoughts. "Please help me understand. You are the one secretly working in the gardens and you also know Farfar's plans?"

"Of course, that's a house elf's job! It's a matter of pride with us."

"Oh, oh, I see your farfar heading this way. The gig is up. He will see me because, of course, he also ate the honey. I've tried to avoid him too, but I guess it's time we all got acquainted."

"Punzel, I wondered where you had gone off to." Her grandfather arrived carrying a mug of steaming coffee. "Who have you found to talk with so early in the morning?"

"Oh, Farfar, I have found Alf's tomte. Tomtar really do exist! Please come and meet one."

"Now, YOU are pulling my leg!" He loved to tease Punzel. But when he saw Pung he did not appear to be as astonished as his granddaughter had been. Pung's size was what interested Arne the most. Pung's head barely reached above Arne's knees. He knelt down to get a better look at the remarkable little man.

"Well, well, well, we finally meet." Arne held out on his hand. "I'm very glad to make your acquaintance at last." As the small hand touched the larger, Punzel's expression changed to amazement. "You mean, you knew about Pung?"

"I suspected someone of the sort," answered her grandfather. "You remember all the references to 'we' in my bror's journal? I figured it was someone Alf discovered while learning about his enchanted land. I was pretty sure Alf wasn't carrying a mouse around in his pocket. And I didn't think magic kept Alf's cottage clean after his absence."

"Oh, my goodness!" Punzel jumped up. "Farfar, I just remembered! I kept forgetting to tell you about the little furniture in the loft by the chimney where I found Alf's journal.

"Pung, that's your furniture!" Punzel clapped her hands and looked at the elf with satisfaction.

"I knew you were smart!" Pung beamed. "Now that you have found me out, can I move back into the cottage? When I saw you eating the magical honey, I knew I had to hide or you would see me. I'm tired of sleeping in the shed and then hiding from the big guy when he works in there." He directed his gaze at Arne.

"Of course you can stay with us. The cottage is really more your home than ours. I hope we will become friends. Alf was certainly fortunate to have a companion like you. And one that can keep secrets. Right Pung?" There followed a wink by the big guy and a nod by the smaller.

"I don't know what you two are gesturing about, but I do know I'm hungry. Would both of you like breakfast?" invited Punzel turning toward the little cottage. "I made some pancake batter yesterday. They can be ready in a jiffy."

Eagerly, the tall and the short followed the young woman, one step of Arne's equaling three of Pung's. The extinguished lantern swung to and fro as the elf ran to keep up with the man's long, swift strides. That night the little furniture in the loft was once again in use and Punzel dreamt of the magic of the Tidendal Woods.

Chapter 4
Into the Tidendal Woods

Some miles away from Alf's homestead and months before Punzel and Arne's arrival, a mysterious and frightening illness was spreading among the woodland creatures.

The warm fingers of the early spring sun reached through the budding branches of the forest, gently prodding the animals and plants to awaken to the rites of nature's renewal. Snow drops, always the most anxious of spring flowers, poked their dainty heads through the warming soil to greet the new season. They heard the sounds of busy saws and hammers as the woodlanders repaired dwellings damaged by winter. Dainty curtains and linens flapped in the crisp breeze as spring house cleaning was in evidence throughout the land. No self-respecting person, or creature, would think of playing before house duties were completed.

Along the forest riverbank, tufts of grass turned from light to dark green, enriched by the sun's vital rays. The river flowed swiftly over gravel and logs and slithered around huge rocks and sandbars, carving a serpentine trail through the stirring forest. At one bend, a collection of fallen logs calmed the churning water. Anchored to these logs was a network of branches that gave shelter to a colony of green frogs. Torv, a teenage member of the colony, was hopping along the beach picking up twigs. He stopped when he saw his friend Lucia trip over a tree root. She blinked her large round eyes at him and plopped down on a rock.

"I'm not paying much attention to what I'm doing this morning,"

Lucia muttered. "I guess it's because I have a lot on my mind. My aunt hasn't been feeling well. Last night I talked with Maria and Rose. They said their parents have stomach aches like my aunt. It's beginning to sound like an epidemic, but none of us younger frogs are sick. I wonder why?"

Torv dropped his pile of twigs and sat down beside her. "Even though we are small, we are the first to notice when something in the river isn't right. Let's ask the otters if they have heard of any sickness in other frog colonies. They travel further along the river."

"Oh, that's a good idea," Lucia replied.

Then, suddenly Lucia threw up her arms. "I've got it! Something in the water could be making the older frogs ill. Oh, what's next! It's bad enough living close to a couple of blue herons. She isn't too bad, but he's a rogue. He stands on that sand bar so quiet and still, pretending that he's looking for a nice fat, juicy fish. Then, ZAP! He grabs one of us. He has NO conscience at all!"

"Look, here comes Bertil." Torv stood up and waved. "Maybe he can tell us what's happening to our elders. Uh, oh, he looks kind of excited." The river otter's sleek head broke the water's surface and he bounded onto the bank near Torv's pile of twigs. "What's the matter, Bertil?" asked Torv.

"I have bad news." The tawny otter shook his head. "The older frogs are sick in the colony by the tannery. They have been poisoned! Is anyone ill in your colony?"

"Yes," they cried. "Many of our elders are sick. Are they being poisoned, too?"

Usually otters find frogs to be a good dietary choice, but after Lucia and Torv had warned Bertil and his friends about traps hidden in the shallow waters along the river bank, they became heroes and Bertil removed frogs from his menu.

"Yes. I think food poisoning is most likely the cause of their illness and that tannery is responsible," Bertil scratched his head. "The tannery uses strong chemicals to process leather. The acid waste from those chemicals was dumped onto the ground last fall and it seeped into the river water this spring. The insects in the water have absorbed the poison and then the frogs eat the insects. If your elders are sick, the poison has already traveled this far from the tannery. I must find out what food is poisoning the older frogs and swim downriver to warn others of the danger."

"I knew it was something in the water!" Lucia jumped up ready for action. "We want to go with you. Let us tell the others and then we will be right back." Torv nodded in agreement.

"Okay, but please hurry," urged Bertil. "I have a feeling we're already too late to help any water creature that lives downriver from the tannery."

Bertil's news spread like wildfire and before long Lucia and Torv were back, along with several of their friends. The young frogs had asked their parents for permission to go along and Ralph, Torv's friend, told Bertil, "My father said that the spitting wattle bugs have had a very odd flavor this spring and they are a favorite of many older frogs."

"Well, I'll be!" Torv did a backward flip. "They must have poison in them. All we have to do is taste the spitting wattle bugs and if they taste bad, we'll know how far the poison has spread."

"That's a good idea, Torv," praised Ralph. "But we must warn everyone to spit them out after tasting them or we will get sick too." The spitting wattle bug would be their test of safe water.

Bertil and the abler older frogs promptly constructed two twig rafts, each woven with wood vine. All agreed that using rafts to float with the river's current would save their energy for the return swim home. Meanwhile, the young frogs found strong sticks to act as rudders and packed baskets with dried bugs from the winter's storage. They weren't taking any chances on river food. By late morning the rafts were finished. As soon as the food baskets were secured, the sailors pushed off from shore and the rafts were immediately swept into the river's current. Shouts from shore carried wishes for a safe journey and a speedy return.

Each frog took his or her turn as raft captain. Steering was great fun! Ralph commanded the lead raft and Lucia captained the other. Torv lounged. He was delighted with this mode of transportation, as he was partial to dry feet. Torv was known in frog circles as "not the most energetic." Drifting and dreaming was just his style. When he did get a notion to work, he tended to be headstrong and prone to act on impulse. Lucia was the opposite. She was of a thoughtful, serious nature. She had proven to be a diligent worker and was, despite her young age, a respected colony member. Bertil was the prankster, always ready for adventure and a good time, but he was, for all his spirit, a true and loyal friend.

The rafts would steer to the side of the river for the taste test whenever spitting wattle bugs were sighted. The answer was always the same: "These bugs taste yucky!" After a while the wattle bug sightings grew fewer and raft travel became monotonous. Bertil, never one to be bored, would swim below the rafts to investigate shadowy rocks surrounded by waterborne roots and undulating vegetation. His intrusion sent schools of small fish or minnows into hiding.

In mid afternoon, the river knifed through a tunnel of branches. Inspired by Bertil, the shipmates decided to make up a game of their own.

"Last one through the tunnel is a toad," croaked Torv.

Suddenly the rafts were transformed into centipedes as every frog took up the challenge. Webbed feet splashed from the sides and rear. Even Torv's feet could be seen flapping in the water. Ralph's raft was in the lead at first, then Lucia's raft took the lead. Excitement abounded! However, the race came to an abrupt end as the tunnel narrowed. Bong! The rafts collided sending everyone sprawling. Arms and legs bumped heads and bodies. After untangling themselves and checking the food baskets, they found that all was intact. All agreed that it had been a great game and declared the race a tie. (Young ones on a serious mission sometimes need to bolster their spirits with a good diversion.)

Beyond the tunnel the river broadened and flowed at a more leisurely pace. The gentle motion invited the weary sailors to stretch out and relax in the late afternoon sunshine. Soon they fell asleep. Bertil swam for a while, but then he too relaxed and flipped on his backside to float and gaze at the puffy clouds playing tag overhead.

Meanwhile, unseen from the river below, the mischievous, black raven, Kiergaard, hid in the overhead branches of a birch tree. He had spotted the voyagers while hunting and impatiently waited for the rest of his band to join him. When they had assembled, he whispered, "I've spotted a bunch of frogs down on the river. What say we have some sport and give them a good scare?" The ravens' hunt had been successful, leaving them in a good mood. Eager for fun, they nodded in agreement, and when Kiergaard gave the signal, the flock dove toward their quarry. Pandemonium ensued as the startled frogs awoke to the sound of the raven's flapping wings and then the little green bodies leaped into a watery retreat. Sharp claws scratched the twig rafts as the heavy birds tried to land on the small, rocking crafts. Below, the water was charged with foam as the frightened frogs propelled themselves downward toward the safety of the river bottom.

Watching his friends' plight, Bertil yelled at the ravens, trying to distract them, but the ravens were giddy with pleasure and chose to ignore him. Bertil frantically searched for another way to divert their attention. He spied several pebbles on the shore, picked them up in his small paws and hurled them as hard as he could. He hit three marauders and missed two. *Not bad*, he thought, *but I can do better*. He mustered up more energy and let another stone fly. Conk! This rock struck Kiergaard on the side of his head. The blow was too much for the raven leader. Badly shaken, he signaled his band to retreat. The game no longer amused him.

Bertil was jubilant as he watched the ravens fly away. "There they go!" He pounded his chest in jubilation as the young frogs returned to the river's surface. "It was fun seeing them chased away by me, a little otter."

The green chorus echoed his enthusiasm. "Hurrah for Bertil! Thank you for saving us."

"It's all in a journey's work." He smiled a very satisfied smile. "Let's be on our way before they decide to return and give us another try."

As the long shadows of the woods enveloped the light on the river, the adventurers spied a bunch of spitting wattle bugs swimming around a cluster of marsh marigold shoots. Lucia noticed the fading daylight. "This will be our last chance today to know if the poison has spread this far downriver." She snapped up a skittish bug with her graceful tongue. "This tastes no better than the rest." She spit it out in dismay.

Beyond the marigold shoots, they found shelter for the night in a hollow formed by the roots of a gnarled willow. Exhausted and hungry, Bertil invited his friends to sample a stew of steamed roots and lemon grass instead of the dried bugs. To the newly initiated it tasted weird, but they were hungry and ate it all. During the meal, Ralph voiced discouragement.

"We have traveled quite a distance and have found no safe water," Ralph complained. "It seems like the poison is traveling faster than we are. I vote that some of us return home in the morning." It was

29

agreed that Ralph would lead half of the frogs back to their colony and the rest would continue downriver by raft to warn the next frog colony of the poison in the river. Each group would use the shore's cover of dense overhead branches to avoid attracting the ravens. Ralph felt sure they could convince the elder frogs to move their colonies to a site upriver from the tannery where the water would be safe.

Bertil had made his own plans during the night. Over breakfast he told Lucia and Torv that since he no longer had to continue downriver he wanted to look for a new home with clean water elsewhere. Lucia and Torv decided to stay with Bertil. The colony frogs, anxious to get an early start, wished the trio good luck and departed on their separate ways.

Now there was just the three of them and the forest seemed very quiet. "Come on, you two, don't look so glum." Bertil noticed the droopy mouths on his companions. "We have a new journey to begin and I'll bet we make a lot of new friends soon."

Perplexed, Lucia asked, "Which way do we go?"

"I need to get my thinking paws on," laughed Bertil, and he jumped into the river, performing summersaults and flips which brightened the spirits of the onlookers. As he finished one of his tumbling routines, he noticed the woods behind the willow. "Hey, you frogs, stop gawking at me and swim out here and look at what I'm seeing," he commanded.

Torv and Lucia swam to Bertil and looked beyond the willow to the towering spires of majestic pine trees. "Those tall trees are Norwegian pines." Bertil spoke with authority. "Surely, any land that grows such magnificent trees has to be fertile. And look over there!" He waved one paw to the right of the pines. "That looks like a mountain beyond the woods. I hear that many fresh streams flow from a mountain. I vote that we enter this forest and see what it has to offer."

"We agree that you know a lot about a lot of things." Lucia nodded to Torv. "What do you say, Torv? I trust Bertil's judgment. Let's go into the forest with him."

"I hate to give up the raft." Torv glanced at the one left behind and then looked back at the forest. He swallowed. "I kind of hoped we could float a while longer and maybe find a clean stream running into the river." He gave a little frog shrug. "Okay, okay. I'll go with you too, but we'd better find good water soon. Landlubber food is not much better than yucky wattle bugs. And . . . in case you haven't noticed," he looked downward, "we are unlikely pals for a trip over land. These feet are not made for rough woodland ground."

"I'm much better in the water myself," Bertil motioned with a webbed paw, "but we'll have to do the best that we can. You and Lucia can ride on my back. My fur looks sleek in the water, but it has coarse hairs that you will be able to hold on to. We can travel much easier and faster that way."

"Okay, let's try it." Torv's spirits were beginning to brighten at the thought of another ride. "It sounds a lot better than hopping all the way."

"Somehow I knew that would be your answer," replied a smiling Lucia.

"I wish my parents were alive to see me now." Torv splashed and flipped over on his back. "They always thought I was lazy. Well, look at me now! I'm almost grown up, being a teenager is almost grown up, and I'm going on a bigger adventure than they would ever have gone on."

I wish my parents could see me too, thought Lucia. *They would think a trip like this would be dangerous. I'm glad that I have Torv and Bertil as friends, but they sure are different. Torv's parents died in the same mud slide as mine and that made him quite timid like me. Bertil is also an orphan, but he is much bigger and far more bold. He is brave and I know he'll protect us.*

Bertil clambered up the steep river bank followed by Lucia and Torv. They hopped on his back and grabbed onto his coarse hair. "Hey, Bertil, this is pretty neat!" came the excited voice of the teenage green frog as he snuggled into the otter's soft under fur.

The moist uneven forest floor, Bertil's bouncy, clumsy gait, and the fear of spilling his passengers made speed impossible. However, their modest progress had it's bright side. It gave them time to enjoy the beautiful colors of the unfurling foliage—the red of the oak, the yellow of the maple, the light green of the birch. The colors were a vivid contrast to the deep green of the Norwegian Pine. They learned to avoid the bludgeoning thickets of raspberry, gooseberry and blackberry. Birds fluttered to and fro, chirping and busily gathering material for nests, but they also kept a curious eye on the adventurers.

Bertil was about to stop for a rest when a waft of tantalizing odor floated across a grassy knoll and swept toward them on a light spring breeze. "That sure smells like wild leek soup." He sniffed the air and decided to keep going. "What I wouldn't do for a bowl of hot spring tonic."

"I wonder who's making it?" Lucia caught on to Bertil's enthusiasm. On the other side of the knoll they saw a dainty field mouse stirring a metal pot suspended over a low fire.

"Good day," Bertil greeted the little mouse. "I am Bertil and these are my friends Lucia and Torv. We're sorry if we intruded, but we couldn't help following that delicious smell." He nodded wistfully toward the pot.

"Good day to you too," the mouse replied. "My name is Lotta. I didn't realize that my cooking would bring such nice guests. Where are you from?"

"We are from a valley northeast of here," Bertil replied. "The river we came from has become contaminated and we are looking for a new home with clean, fresh water. What is the name of this nice valley?"

"You are in the Tidendal Valley," replied the little mouse. "It is the home of the Tidendal Woods. To the west is Lodespar Mountain."

"Ah." Bertil nodded his head in satisfaction. "I thought I saw a mountain." We would like to settle by a stream that flows from a mountain. Surely it would be clean and good."

"Yes," acknowledged Lotta. "All of the waters in the Tidendal Valley are fed from the pure springs of the Lodespar Mountain, and we woodlanders respect the gifts of nature and take great care to protect them. You all look hungry. May I offer you a bowl of leek soup? Since you liked the smell, maybe you will enjoy the taste."

"We were hoping you would ask," the happy trio answered.

"I have been waiting for the return of my three little ones. They went off to pick fiddlehead ferns for tomorrow's wild asparagus soup. Oh, here they come. They also must have smelled the soup.

"Sara, Sonja, Sofia, I would like you to meet Bertil, Lucia and Torv."

Lotta then told her daughters about the guests' quest.

Bertil was enthralled with their gathering basket. It was filled to the brim with tender fern heads. "You three remind me of me when I was a pup."

Lucia snickered, "Oh, Bertil! You're still a little wet behind the ears." (If a river otter could blush, this was the time.)

"My mom made soup like your mother's," Bertil continued. "She would give me a big basket and send me to dig wild leek roots in the woods by our home. I thought that was a lot of responsibility so I worked very hard to please her. I filled the basket so full that I could barely carry it home. She always rewarded me with a smile and later a big bowl of wild leek soup. That made me very proud."

The savory soup was served in dainty carved bowls, except for Bertil's bowl. It was Lotta's mixing crock, the largest container she could find. "A growing otter like you needs to eat more," she told him kindly.

Lucia noticed that her bowl was intricately carved with forget-me-nots, so she asked Lotta who carved it.

"That bowl is my favorite," was the reply. "It was made by the man who lives at the edge of the forest beside a beautiful heart-shaped pond."

The well-fed trio slept that night in the oak tree house of the little field mouse and her three daughters.

Dawn broke wearing a misty mantle as the travelers bid a reluctant farewell to their gracious hostess and started out in search of the pure waters of Lodespar Mountain. The morning mist made visibility low, so they shared the mood of the forest with imaginary objects. A large lichen-covered rock became a giant toad, some scruffy brush became a haunted hut, and one very tall, pointed stump bore an amazing resemblance to an ancient castle.

Just before noon, as the thick mist started to part, a dark, hunched shape shuffled toward them. Torv and Lucia snuggled deeper into Bertil's fur and Bertil slowed to a crawl. Was this a real being or another fantasy? The source of their anxiety drifted closer and closer. It was poking and waving a stick and carrying a sack of some kind. Then, before they thought of running, the sun broke through the last of the fog and there, bathed in sunlight, stood an old badger, glaring at them.

"Whew, I was really getting a little nervous," whispered Torv to Bertil. "Weren't you?"

"Naw," came the reply. "I knew who it was all along. It takes a lot more than an old badger to scare me."

To show that he hadn't been frightened, Bertil ambled over to the badger and greeted him. "Hi," said the brave otter. "We are on our way to find the pure waters of Lodespar Mountain. Are we heading in the right direction?"

"You sure are, sonny." The old badger paused and leaned on his stick. "I'm surprised to see young folk like you out on a morning like this."

"We have to find a new home." Torv was back to his old self. "We watched you bending over and waving that stick. What were you doing?"

"Don't you dare tell anyone where you've seen me," the old badger gruffly replied. "I'm hunting morel mushrooms. No one ever tells where they find them. I have my favorite spots. They would not be secret any more, if you tell."

"Oh, we promise not to tell," said a sincere Lucia looking closely at his sack. "Do you always put them in that mesh pouch? And how do you find them in the first place? They certainly blend in with the ground."

"My, you do ask a lot of questions." The badger had a stern face but there was a twinkle in his eyes. "I will tell you, since you promised not to tell where I found them. I walk very slowly and carefully so as not to step on any mushrooms I haven't seen. Morels are very elusive. The hunter has to be patient and keep a sharp lookout for unusual leafy mounds. When I find one, I gently lift the mound with my walking stick and, if I'm lucky, a little morel will be underneath. Presto! I pop it into my pouch and then I continue looking for its friends. Where there is one, there are generally more. Did I answer all of your questions?"

"Just one more, please," begged Lucia. "I can't help but admire your walking stick carved with all sorts of mushrooms and vines. Where did you get it? It looks like it was made for you."

"Ah, you are indeed right, little one," the badger nodded with pleasure. "This staff was made especially for me by the man who lives at the edge of the forest beside a beautiful heart-shaped pond."

Lucia smiled, "We have heard of this man before. He must be very well known."

"Yes, he is somewhat of a legend. I heard tell stories of how he saved many a woodlander from serious accident. If you ever meet up with him, know that you have met a great man. Now I had better be on my way. My wife expects me to be back for dinner with my pouch filled. Good luck on finding your new home." And the old badger disappeared into the brush as though he had evaporated.

"We had better be off," announced Bertil. "At least we know we are heading in the right direction."

34

The night was warm, the sky clear. They fell asleep counting stars after they snuggled into a bed of soft leaves. (Lucia did check to see if the leaf mounds hid any morels before they could lie down.)

Morning sleep did not want to leave Bertil and Lucia, but Torv was ready for action as the first light of day peered through the trees. He had spent most of the night dreaming of fairy shrimp chowder. *I'm sick of this landlubber food*, he thought. *I'm going to find good water with decent frog food. I know the direction we're taking. I'll just hop ahead for a little bit. Ha! Won't they be surprised that I'VE found good water. Then they'll think I'm really growing up.*

Sprong! Sprong! Sprong! Torv flew over the ground in giant hops! Soon he noticed the ground getting wetter and wetter. Encouraged by the sight of sprouting cattails, the impetuous frog made one last gigantic leap, confident his landing would be in clear water. Plunk! Instead he landed in a mucky, dark ooze! Then, he began to sink!

Okay Torv, he told himself. *Calm down and think. What does a young, green frog do in a emergency? He screams!*

With that Torv let out a scream the likes of which the Tidendal Woods had never heard.

Chapter 5
Quest for a New Home

Torv's shrill screams woke up not only Bertil and Lucia, but also Jarl, a swashbuckling red squirrel.

"Who's making that racket?" Jarl yelled down from his overnight lodging in a tall oak tree. "Is there no such thing as QUIET anywhere? A poor soul just can't get a good night's sleep any more," he grumbled to himself. "What's this forest coming to?"

Bertil, with Lucia on his back, bounded from their cozy bed of warm leaves toward the shouts and screams. They were sure something awful had happened to Torv because they found only the boisterous squirrel, chattering his displeasure.

"Where is Torv?" Bertil interrupted as he frantically searched the ground near the oak tree.

"How should I know?" came the angry reply from above. "I was trying to get my much needed, well deserved rest when I was awakened by horrible earsplitting noises. Nearly scared me to death. Who is this Torv?"

"He's our friend, a green frog like me," replied Lucia. "I know he's in trouble because when we're scared, we make shrill screechy sounds."

Another scream pierced the air.

"It's Torv! We must help him." Lucia hopped from Bertil's back and sprang in the direction of Torv's scream. Bertil started to follow, but the ground became waterlogged and each paw sunk deeper and deeper into the thick black ooze.

"You'd better wait there," Lucia directed. "You're too heavy for this mud or whatever it is." She too began to sink as she spied Torv's head through the cattail sprouts. "Stop yelling and squirming, you little green blob! You're just digging yourself in further. We'll find a way to get you out."

Desperate, she hopped back to Bertil and the disgruntled squirrel. "Torv is being sucked up in that awful, black slime. We can't reach him by land. That muck won't support my weight either. Please Sir Squirrel, can't YOU do something?"

"First of all, I'm not a sir, although I do rather like the meaning. Secondly, I don't do anything strenuous before breakfast, which I haven't as yet eaten. Thirdly, I don't know either of you."

"Excuse me. I'm Bertil, and this is my friend Lucia. I apologize for our lack of manners, but you MUST understand that we are upset about our companion's plight. Our friend Torv has a habit of getting himself into predicaments, I'm afraid."

"Yes, yes, I understand." The red squirrel had calmed down. "My name's Jarl. I've spent the last week climbing on Lodespar Mountain. Keeps me physically fit, don't you see." He flexed his muscles. "Oh, well, I can't deny a fellow in need. Let me think what to do."

"Please, sir—I mean Jarl—please think fast. Torv's not a patient frog and I'm afraid he will wiggle so much that he'll suffocate himself," cried Lucia.

"Chrrrrrrrrr. Stifle the tears, my lady. As tired as I am, a plan is forming. Do you see that long limb on my oak tree? It should reach to just above your friend's head. Lucky for him I have my climbing rope handy. I can make a loop in one end of the rope and lower it down from that limb. Torv can slip the loop under his arms and together Bertil and I should be able to pull him up."

The bushy-tailed squirrel, true to his word, got Torv to calm down and put his arms through the loop of the dangling rope while Bertil held fast to the other end. Then, on Jarl's signal they pulled. Whoosh! Torv was hoisted out of the slime and onto a high, grassy mound. Never had he been so glad to feel solid ground! A very shaky, grateful frog thanked the ingenious squirrel and introduced himself.

Jarl, won over by Torv's gratitude, invited the threesome to share his breakfast. They dined on cereal made from dried blueberries, crunchy walnuts and wild wheat berries topped with yummy sweet cream and ate oat biscuits spread with lingonberry jam. Jarl was a very resourceful squirrel. This was one landlubber meal Torv was grateful to eat!

"Where did you get such delicious jam?" Lucia daintily wiped her mouth with a soft bit of moss. "I've never tasted berries quite like these."

"The jam was a gift from the man who lives at the edge of the forest beside a beautiful heart-shaped pond."

During breakfast, the travelers explained their quest to find a home near clear, fresh water. Jarl told them about a beaver family that lived in Leaning Tree Pond. "They know all the waterways in the valley, and I'm sure they'll give you the best advice." He gave them directions for a safe route, which circumvented the boggy flat-land. Their stomachs full, Bertil thanked Jarl for his hospitality and started down the path to the beavers' lodge.

"Say hello to Ragnar and Gabriella Beaver for me," Jarl called after them as they neared the first bend.

The trio traveled under an emerging network of leaves. "Look at these sweet flowers." Lucia pointed to the delicate pink and blue buttercups that seemed to be waiting for the overhead foliage to catch up. Shafts of sunlight focused on the stately posture of white, pink and red trillium. Downy yellow violets waved a greeting as the explorers passed by. Bertil was also captivated by the exuberant spring flowers, pausing often to sniff their fragrance and enjoy the many floral faces. The Tidendal Woods was an exciting world for two of the brave adventurers.

Torv didn't join in their enthusiasm. "Can't we just keep going?" he would wail. "When you've seen one violet, you've seen them all. My skin is stiff as a board from this dry, scratchy mud and itches like a horsehair blanket. Oh, for the chance to dive into fresh water."

"I can't believe what I just heard." Lucia looked up from examin-ing a flower that looked like little yellow pants. "Maybe there is hope for you as a frog yet."

Bertil, always ready for a joke, teased, "Torv, hasn't your impetu-ousness taught you to have a little more patience? The next time you won't do something the rest of us would like to do, I'm going to call you an old 'stick in the mud.'" Lucia tried hard to hide a smile.

They arrived at Leaning Tree Pond in time to watch the sun cast long shadows from the surrounding pines onto its tranquil waters. "Make way!" Torv's ardent cry was accompanied by a muddy streak that cracked the pond's mirrored surface. Kerplunk! This time his leap had landed him in fresh, clear water—and over the head of a very surprised beaver.

"Here we go again," Bertil whispered to Lucia. "What do you think about our chances of a friendly reception?"

To their astonishment and relief, the beaver surfaced laughing. "That must have been Torv. Hi! I'm Ragnar. You must be Bertil and Lucia. Welcome to Leaning Tree Pond. This is my wife, Gabriella. We have been expecting you."

"Hello." Bertil and Lucia said as one and bowed their heads.

"Please pardon Torv's impatience," Lucia explained. "He has been through a difficult time."

Bertil could hardly wait to dive into the water himself, but curiosity got the best of him. "How did you know we were coming?"

"Gerda, the gyrfalcon, was kind enough to fly over and tell us," Ragnar replied. "Gerda is most helpful in delivering messages between woodlanders."

"You trust a gyrfalcon?" Bertil shuttered. "I've heard that they are huge dangerous birds who carry off small woodland animals in their great claws."

"Yes, that's true of most gyrfalcons, but Gerda has learned the ways of the Tidendal Woods. When you hear her story you will understand our friendship."

"I hope that day doesn't come too soon," replied a doubtful Lucia.

Torv joined the group, giving Ragnar the opportunity to change the subject. "My, you must be hungry. Come to our home and meet Gabriella, she has prepared a fine meal."

The water loving animals swam toward the beaver's lodge, a huge mound of mud-mortared limbs and branches in the middle of Leaning Tree Pond. They dove underwater following Ragnar through the lodge's watery entrance. Cozy lantern light embraced them as they were greeted by a cheerful lady beaver. Behind her apron poked the heads of three shy pups and seated at the table were two older siblings. Ragnar introduced his wife, Gabriella, and his five off-spring.

"Please join us for dinner and stay here tonight," said the cheerful hostess. "Our lodge is quite large and includes several guest rooms. You don't need to feel like you're imposing," she continued, as she saw Bertil about to object. "We welcome company. Many friends stay with us as they travel the forest."

The hungry guests enjoyed a large plateful of water lily shoots and minnows. Then to Torv's delight, Gabriella served a soup made with water striders, back swimmers, and dragonfly larva, plus a side bowl of fairy shrimp. Torv was so ecstatic, his bulging eyes flashed red. The dessert of petite cattail flour cookies embossed with woodland flower designs captivated Lucia.

"These are the loveliest cookies I've ever seen." She thought them too pretty to eat. "May I ask how you got those designs in the cookies?"

"I'm glad you like them." Gabriella beamed with pride. "Making designs in the cookies is easy. A friend of ours, the man that lives at the edge of the woods beside a beautiful heart-shaped pond, carved designs in a rolling pin he made for me. I roll the pin over the dough and a carved design appears on each cookie."

"We've heard of this man from the woodlanders we've met on our journey to find a new home. Would it be possible to meet him?" Lucia was determined to find the legendary woodsman.

"My, yes. The distance isn't far," replied Gabriella. "We can ask Gerda to guide you when she stops by."

After the young beavers were put to bed, the rest relaxed with cups of cowslip tea and a mouth-watering strawberry sponge cake. The adventurers told of the poison in their homeland river, their raft trip, and their travels through the Tidendal Woods. Ragnar and Gabriella were horrified to hear of the ruined waterway and the blight of the creatures who lived in and along its banks.

"We don't allow anyone to pollute our water or damage our woods," stated Ragnar.

"Alf, the man who carved Gabriella's rolling pin, helps Gunvald Moose and Gerda protect the forest and Lodespar Mountain. We all want the Tidendal Valley to remain clean and beautiful. We also are a peace-loving community, but of course we have our disagreements. If you have thoughts of living in this forest, you must know that we do have our 'different' sorts," added Gabriella, "but we respect the individual's rights and we resolve our differences."

"These are no ordinary woods or mountain." Ragnar added. "Lodespar Mountain is the home of an ancient clan of silversmiths. They are trolls who have lived there for thousands of years and are very territorial, loud and cantankerous. Sometimes they visit the forest and disturb our peace. We accept them, but we prefer the gentle elves who are good friends. They live throughout the Tidendal

Woods and come often to Leaning Tree Pond.

"You have a lot to learn, if you decide to stay in this forest," Ragnar concluded. "We'll let you get your rest tonight and tomorrow you'll learn more."

Sleep that night was filled with pleasant dreams as the weary travelers, glad to have finally reached a land of clean pure water, relaxed and reveled in peaceful slumber.

The next morning, the loud flapping of wings brought the inhabitants out of the beavers' lodge and into the bright morning light. Gerda Gyrfalcon had returned to Leaning Tree Pond! The sight of Gerda's huge beak and monstrous talons sent shivers down the spines of Lucia, Torv and Bertil as they crouched at the water's edge.

"You need not fear Gerda," reassured Ragnar and Gabriella. The three beaver pups scooted over to Gerda and cuddled under her resting wings to show there was no danger.

Ragnar introduced Gerda to Lucia, Bertil and Torv. "They have traveled from a contaminated river to the north in search of a new home with fresh water." One glance told Ragnar that the newcomers were still very apprehensive about Gerda. Even the brave river otter was reluctant to join in conversation with the large bird.

Gerda tried to reassure them with her gentle ways. "I've heard stories of the bad water in the river to the north. We've been fortunate to live on land protected from disasters like that."

Gerda turned to Ragnar and Gabriella. "I bring you terrible news. Yesterday I flew over Alf's cottage and I saw his elf, Pung, coming out of their shed. He told me Alf had passed away. I'm so sad. He was such a good friend to all of us."

Gabriella sobbed, "What a fine man. We'll really miss him."

"What will happen to our forest now that Alf has gone?" Gabriella was concerned about her family's welfare.

"Pung said Alf's brother will inherit the land." Gerda replied. "We shall have to be patient until he arrives."

"Let's hope Alf's brother is as kind as he was." Gabriella tried to put a hopeful smile on her face for the sake of her guests and the young ones. Then she asked Gerda. "Please tell our new friends the story of how Alf saved your life."

Gerda nodded and directed her attention to the travelers. "Perhaps my story will help you understand that you have nothing to fear from me."

"In my young life," Gerda began, "I was a rambunctious fledgling proud of my ancestry. After all, my great, great, great-grandfather was raised by King Gustavus Vasa of Sweden and several of my great aunts and uncles were bred by other kings and noblemen of the North Lands as well. We were known as 'The Great Hunters.'" Gerda expanded her chest. "My parents came to this forest with the first settlers. Because of my heritage I thought I was entitled to behave in an arrogant manner. I flew the forest watching the small woodland creatures cower when I came near. I felt my power and used it. No eyes were keener than mine, no talon sharper.

"One day I spotted a young beaver by a log dam. I swooped to capture her and instead I became the captive. My right claw got trapped between two logs as they shifted in the river's flow. The beaver got away, but the logs held me fast and I was certain starvation was to be my end. During those dire days, I reassessed my short life. I had done no great deeds like my ancestors. I had only incurred the fear and loathing of the other creatures of the forest. Was this to be my legacy? Would I not live long enough to see my fledglings born?

"Finally, I decided that, if by some miracle I lived, I would change my life around and be a kind caring gyrfalcon. I would set an example for other creatures both on wing and on paw. No sooner had I settled in my resolve when there appeared a woodsman accompanied by an elf.

"Luckily the pair spotted me, as I had no strength of voice left. They worked as a team. The woodsman wielded his ax and the elf cleared the chopped logs. They carried me to a cottage at the edge of the woods beside a beautiful heart-shaped pond and cared for me.

"As I grew in strength, I told my story and thanked them for saving my life. They showed me what real kindness was. I felt ashamed of my former lifestyle and was more determined than ever to become a worthy creature.

"Since that incident, I have mated and raised three families of gyrfalcons. All of my fledglings know my story and have vowed to live their lives as I have. My mate has taken the same vow. We are proud to be among the peaceful creatures of this valley."

"That's a wonderful story," Lucia, Torv and Bertil agreed. Their fear had vanished.

"What Gerda didn't tell you is that I was that young beaver on the dam," explained Gabriella. "We both have much to be grateful for."

"My right claw remains crippled from the accident," Gerda raised her damaged claw, "but it serves as a reminder of my old ways. I'm still strong of wing and can do much to help others. I will continue to repay my debt to Alf."

Lucia and Bertil told Gerda they wanted to visit Alf's cottage and meet Pung. "He's probably very sad," said Lucia. We might cheer him up with stories of the creatures we have met who admire Alf. Would you please guide us?"

Gerda was on an errand for a group of hedgehogs living near Lodespar Mountain. She left with the promise that she would return and guide them to Pung and the heart-shaped pond.

•   •   •   •   •

The mood of the Leaning Tree Pond population was very somber for the next few days. Everyone felt the loss of Alf. Bertil, Lucia and Torv agreed to accept the beavers' kind invitation to stay with them until Gerda's return.

As early summer descended, Torv developed an interest in sailing and was content to whirl around the pond on his chosen "lily pad of the day." He developed a technique in steering the shiny pads that was admired by the other frogs. "Torv is becoming quite a sailor," was commonly heard among the local pond dwellers. But occasionally his ego got wounded. Sometimes he would skim over the water, wind in his maple leaf sail, then suddenly the wind would shift leaving his "boat" facing the wind. That maneuver would cause his lily pad boat to sail backwards and give his admirers a good laugh. Torv didn't like being laughed at.

One summer day, Torv drifted to sleep with the sail secured by a vine to his right foot. Suddenly a gust of wind jerked the sail across the lily pad throwing Torv into the water. He came up sputtering. That time he didn't have an audience, for which he was immensely grateful.

While Torv enjoyed the sporting life, Lucia was busy learning the culinary arts. She wanted to be a hostess like Gabriella. Gabriella's refreshing pond spritzers (fresh berries plus fizzy water) and her cattail flour cookies were sought after by every visitor. Lucia learned to bake Water's Edge Scones and a yummy Harvest Pudding. From the Forest Animal's Recipe Exchange she found Bjorn Bear's Apple Cake recipe made with dried apples, honey and crunchy walnuts. She would serve that first when she moved into her new home. On a particularly hot day in June the cooks made chilled Ansa Duck's

43

Soup, which brought rave reviews, but the accompaniment, a flavorful cheese cracker, caused the most commotion. Torv said the crackers looked like toad skins. He thought toads need recognition, too! Everyone roared and croaked with laughter.

Bertil had a different way of passing the time before Gerda's return. Bertil loved to pick berries and Gabriella always had a treat of caramelized hazel nuts waiting for him when he returned with his fruit-laden baskets. One early July morning, Bertil's hunt for the best berries turned into the discovery of another secret of the Tidendal Woods. He found a huge berry patch at the edge of a woodland clearing. He was so busy picking the ripe juicy raspberries that he didn't notice large gray clouds roll overhead. Startled by the big raindrops bouncing off his nose he bounded for shelter. He spied a hollow between two beech tree roots and crawled inside. The baskets safe, he curled up and was soon fast asleep.

Bertil awoke to singing. The rain had stopped and the air was full of the sweet smell of freshly washed greens and summer flowers. He looked in the direction of the music and rubbed his eyes in amazement. In the clearing a group of red hatted men and women, barely two feet tall and clothed in muted colors of brown, gray and green, danced in a circle around a ring of beautiful white daisies. The daisies swayed to the music and nodded to the hundreds of mushrooms growing beside them in the lush green grass.

Why they're not much taller than me! Bertil watched, transfixed, as the dancers sang and held hands while circling the daisies. Faster and faster they moved, their heels flying until their feet no longer touched the ground. Finally, out of breath they collapsed on the soft grass, laughing. The spell broken, Bertil approached them. "Hi, I'm Bertil. I've been enjoying your singing and dancing. I've never seen woodlanders like you. What species are you?"

"Hello, Bertil. I'm Enok, the lead elf," came the reply. "We are forest elves who help the animals and care for the forest by planting flowers and young trees. There are forty seven of us throughout the Tidendal Woods.

"You are so small to do so much work," praised the amazed otter.

"Oh, we are quite strong despite our size. Our looks may be deceiving," Enok emphasized. "But of course, we aren't as strong as Pung."

"My friends are I are going to visit Pung as soon as Gerda Gyrfalcon returns." Bertil acknowledged with satisfaction.

"We had heard that you and your friends are staying with Ragnar and Gabriella Beaver. You'll enjoy meeting Pung. He's a good house elf and looks a lot like us, but is a third taller and can lift a log that would take three of us. We were sorry to hear that Pung's master, Alf, passed away this spring." Enok bowed his head for a moment. "Alf was a friend to all of us. He discovered us over three and one half decades ago when he fell into one of our magic daisy rings. Otherwise only animals and other magical creatures can see us.

"We want Pung to live in the forest with us, but he's waiting to see if Alf's brother will come from the faraway land. We try to visit him as often as we can to keep him from feeling too lonely.

"That berry is a favorite of Gabriella's and one of our best experiments." Enok noticed Bertil's baskets. "We also developed the brambleberry, a cross between a grape, a blackberry and an almond as a gift to Alf. Very berry good," he giggled. "When you visit the heart-shaped pond you'll see the brambleberry bushes at the foot of the bridge. Try them. That is, if you can ever find any ripe ones." Enok let out a knowing chuckle. "They seem to have a way of disappearing." The other elves chuckled their agreement.

"It was a pleasure chatting with you," Bertil nodded to the little elves. "I want Lucia and Torv to meet you. Torv is a little different, but a good friend."

"We are all a little different. We look forward to our next meeting with your friends. Your visit will be good for Pung. See you later."

Then they vanished with a POOF!

First you see them, then you don't. Bertil was still in a bit of a daze. *They're here, then they aren't. Fascinating! They must be the friendly elves the beavers were talking about. Now I wonder what trolls are like? Well, I'd better get back to the lodge before they send out a search party for me. I can't wait to tell them who I met.*

Bertil's adventure brought many questions from Torv and Lucia. Lucia was more anxious than ever to meet Pung and see the heart-shaped pond. Torv reluctantly agreed to go with them, but he was

45

not looking forward to another jaunt through the forest nor a chance meeting with little folk in pointed red hats.

The third week in July, Gerda arrived. There had been a big hub-bub at Lodespar Mountain delaying her return. "It was nothing unusual," she explained. "The trolls love to argue and sometimes their disagreements cause a commotion in the forest as well. This time it was the younger trolls who took advantage of their parents distraction and started chasing the smallest hedgehogs, chipmunks, squirrels and rabbits and scattered them in all directions. The elder woodlanders had to rely on my sharp eyes to find the missing young ones.

"The dispute was so bad that Gunvald Moose had to be called in to settle it. No troll defies Gunvald. It was fun to see the old boy in action, antlers at the ready, eyes flashing! Those trolls are just big bullies when it comes down to it. They didn't want the embarrass-ment of Gunvald hooking them on his antlers and carrying them to a cooling-off spot, so they readily agreed to keep better watch over their young ones. That won't last for long. Those young trolls are trouble makers."

Torv didn't want to hear any more about trolls. "When do we leave?" He turned to Lucia. "I'd just as soon stay here but seeing as you two are determined to go, let's get on with it!"

Over a wonderful dinner of watercress soup and carrot bread, it was planned that they would begin the last leg of their journey at dawn. Appetites satisfied, they retired early in anticipation of the next day's journey.

The next day, the cool morning air inspired the travelers to pro-ceed at a fast clip. Gerda held a steady course from the air, guiding her land-anchored companions along the easiest course possible. After an hour of brisk travel, Bertil raised a paw signaling Gerda for a rest. Gerda obliged with a steep dive and landed in a clearing in front of them.

"Sorry for the fast pace," she apologized. "I don't know 'slow,' but you managed to keep up Bertil. You're a good 'bounder.'"

"Thank you." Bertil beamed. "I'm faster in the water! I worry that my bouncing makes it hard for Lucia and Torv to hang on."

"Aye," replied Torv, "I almost lost my skin back there. I think I have fur burn and whiplash."

"We're almost to Alf's cottage," encouraged Gerda. "I'll leave you here. Just follow the path and you'll soon be there."

Gerda flew off to pick up and deliver some river roots to an ailing muskrat and Bertil began to amble (a slow leisurely gait) down the path while his topside passengers relaxed their tired muscles and breathed sighs of relief. The trio, happy to be nearing their destination, enjoyed greeting the many woodland creatures that paused to give them a nod of the head or wave of the paw. "I think this is certainly a very friendly place," observed Bertil. "Fox and rabbit, possum and mouse seem to respect each other. I think..."

"Look," interrupted Torv, stretching up as high as he could from his vantage point on Bertil's head. "I see a pond and beyond is a cottage."

Torv leaped toward the crystal clear water of the heart-shaped pond. Croaking his pleasure, he shot like an arrow onto a layer of velvety lily pads. Bertil followed closely behind. His own entry style was a slide down a smooth, steeply-sloped bank. "Whee!" he shouted as he skittered down the sandy chute. SPLASH! Into the water he plunged! "Yippee! What a great place! Come on in Lucia! The water's super!"

Lucia, knowing Bertil's enthusiasm for water, had jumped to safety before he hit the slide. She was about to join her frolicking friends when a deep, booming voice rang out across the pond.

"WHO DARES DISTURB MY SLEEP!"

Chapter 6
A Solitary Creature

WHO DARES DISTURB MY SLEEP!" repeated the deep voice from below the wooden bridge.

The joyous croaks and cheers from Torv and Bertil as they splashed in the clear waters of the beautiful heart-shaped pond were silenced by the angry tone. Startled, the swimmers froze motionless while Lucia leaped behind a rock. Her large, bulging eyes were fixed on the curtain of moonflower vines as it parted. From the shadows of the pond's wooden bridge, a being emerged: Drekel the troll—and in the worst of his foul moods!

Mangy coarse hair enveloped the creature's body except for his pale wrinkled face, his long gnarled three-fingered hands and his four-toed feet. Pointed ears poked through the massive hair. But the most amazing, show-stopping, spectacular spectacle was the flowers. Entwined with wood vine, a cloud of blooms surrounded the crown of his head and dangled like exotic rope tresses to the knob of his cow-like tail. There were white violets, blue violets, pink violets, and yellow violets. There were dandelions, daisies, forget-me-nots, columbine, yellow and pink ladies' slippers, delicate blue phlox and a multitudinous variety of pansies that vibrated like they were in continuous conversation with each other. Except for his bombastic booming voice and dark beady eyes, the cacophony of shapes and colors made the creature look more like a huge bouquet that had sprouted hands and feet.

•   •   •   •   •

Drekel was a troll—a troll who was enamored of the wild flowers, berry bushes, vines, and trees of the Tidendal valley. Trolls are notori-

48

ously dirty and Drekel was no exception. The accumulation of soil in his massive gray hair attracted and nurtured many wood vines and wildflowers. They grew and flourished year round, protected by his shaggy mane. The most notable evidence that Drekel had become as one with the forest was a handsome juniper tree that grew on Drekel's impressively long nose. He was particularly fond of this tree as he could see it at all times, especially when he crossed his close set, beady dark eyes. Elliptical ears, resembling the leaves of the white ash, pierced Drekel's hair, ending in points that changed from light green to purple. His rope-like tail terminated in a hairy knob that dragged behind him, churning leaves and small pebbles as he clomped through the underbrush.

Drekel was a loner. He wasn't a bad sort, as trolls go, but he went out of his way to avoid contact with any woodland creature. He also steered clear of Alf, but respected the woodsman as a fellow creature who loved the Tidendal Woods. He had first seen the woodsman when Alf was a young man walking through the forest. The troll was startled. His sheltered life in the mountain's caves kept him from contact with creatures from the outside world. "He doesn't have a tail or much hair," he had scoffed. "What kind of beast can that be?"

Drekel also did not understand kindness or goodness, and he certainly didn't want to pay back a "well meant deed." He, in fact, was just plain selfish. Known throughout the forest as the grouchy and very hairy forest fairy, no one dared approach him lest they suffer the consequences of his bad temper. The only life forms which seemed to understand him were the beautiful ever-blooming flowers adorning his mantel of hair. They seemed to revel in their uniqueness. In the warm months, a lean-to of limbs, branches and vines was his temporary forest shelter. Soft woodland moss with a blanket of leaves formed his bed. He traveled the deep woods alone, always alone, looking for a place to call home.

•　　•　　•　　•　　•

Earlier in the spring, when the March snowstorm of 1907 passed into history and the snow on the higher elevations of Lodespar Mountain melted to water and joined the streams that tumbled into the Tidendal Valley below, the woodlanders had disturbed Drekel's peace. Above the sound of the cascading waters Drekel heard the angry shouts of creatures echoing throughout his small cave near the base of Lodespar Mountain.

"Drat their noise!" grumbled the cave's occupant as he paced back and forth, shuffling loose stones with his large, clumsy feet. One hundred years of forest living wasn't time enough to outgrow his early memories. He'd left the raucous inner mountain caverns, at the youthful age of two hundred, to get away from the bickering supervision of his elders and the hard work of mining. But each winter he returned to this cave to rest, tired from roaming the Tidendal Woods in the warmer seasons of spring, summer and fall in search of a permanent home.

He really disliked this shelter. Its unyielding rock and the discordant voices were a reminder of his miserable youth. *I can hardly wait for spring*, he thought. *I'm tired of sleeping on these hard rocks and being awakened by...* His thoughts were interrupted, this time by high-pitched, frightened shouts from the forest outside his cave.

A warm wind ruffled his craggy brow as he peered through the cave's jagged opening searching for the cause of this latest commotion. His eyes squinted at the bright spring sunlight and then focused on the familiar figure of the old woodsman, Alf, trudging across the last patch of snow toward a group of hysterical woodland animals. Drekel had often seen Alf traveling the woodland paths at dusk or in the early morning.

I wonder what those squeaky-voiced woodlanders are all excited about. Drekel tried to discover the cause of their anxiety, but everyone was shouting at the same time. Even the woodsman seemed to have trouble understanding them. *Oh, what nonsense! Just another annoyance! It's time I left this miserable mountain,* he decided, encouraged by the warm spring wind. He scratched around the cave rummaging for his few possessions. Then he filled a coarsely-woven cloth with his meager belongings, tied the corners together, inserted a long sturdy branch through the knot, and balanced the branch on his shoulder with his long three-fingered left hand.

Neither the distraught woodlanders nor the woodsman noticed the cave dweller Drekel as he lumbered across the clearing toward the dense growth of his beloved forest.

In his haste, Drekel had left the cave completely unaware of the direction in which he walked. Nor did he notice his surroundings as he crunched over dried twigs and scuffed up sodden mounds of dead leaves. Sunlight added to his disorientation. (Trolls rarely travel in the light of the noonday sun.) As he trudged along he repeated, "I need to find a home, I need to find a home, I need to find a home."

The forest welcomed the young troll back and saw good in him. "This creature has shown kindness to all living vegetation. Hasn't he suffered enough? Let's give him a test. If he has strength in his heart, he will find his home." Magic spoke to wind, its warm breath cast a trail of snow drops before Drekel. The troll saw them and could hardly believe his good fortune! He followed the path of diminutive flowers, count-ing—counting so many that he lost count. They led to an outcropping of moss-covered rock—a place he recognized but hadn't seen in one hundred years.

The dew-covered moss was soft to his touch as he reached to pull aside meander-ing vines exposing a crevice in the under rock. (No one would believe how gentle Drekel could be.)

"Yes, you are still growing there," he exclaimed in delight. (No one had ever seen his eyes so tender.)

A ray of sunlight spread its countenance on the most beautiful of flowers, now known among botanical connoisseurs as the Troll Flower. The flower's brilliant translucent blue petals were attached to a quivering yellow center that bloomed on a luminous sea green stem. Below the blossom, emer-ald cup-shaped leaves poised to catch moisture from the forest floor. Drekel sat down, as memories of his first sighting of the little flower flooded his mind.

•　　•　　•　　•　　•

For almost two hundred years, Drekel had toiled in the mines where his ancestors had discovered a huge vein of silver that emanated from deep within the bowels of the Lodespar Mountain and spread like branches into smaller veins beneath the Tidendal Woods. One day, Drekel discovered the little Troll Flower while working on one of the smaller veins—his was always the poorest—deep under the forest floor. Working in the narrow confines of the tunnel, he had been startled when a blow of his club exposed a crack in the drift. In the void, he dis-covered this fragile flower nurtured by scant sunlight from the world above. He knew his discovery would remain a secret because no other miner would work on this sparse silver vein. The flower's presence gave him knowledge that beyond the tunnel's rocky barrier was a world where beautiful flowers grew. From that day forward, Drekel yearned to escape the endless corridors of harsh rock illuminated by flickering candlelight casting its meaningless shadows.

As he grew older, Drekel became more of a recluse. His only companion was the little flower. "I promise I will find a way out of this mountain. You have given me hope for a better life," he would say to it. He spoke to no one except the flower. Drekel's quest to reach the outside world wasn't an easy one. The trolls posted guards at all known entrances, no woodlanders were allowed into their mountain and no troll could leave without a pass—those passes were given only to the higher-ranking trolls. Drekel wasn't sure if the guards were posted to protect the silver or keep the laborers from escaping into a kinder, gentler world. For decades, Drekel searched the mountain's many caverns and tunnels, but found no way out.

At last he admitted defeat and asked his only friend, the Troll Flower, if she knew another way he could reach the outside world of growing plants. The Troll Flower listened. She had found him to be of a different nature than the mountain trolls. *Indeed!* the Troll Flower contemplated, *this troll might do well in the world of nature. But he has a lot to learn and it will be a hard life for him there also.*

Drekel fell asleep wondering if the little flower had heard his request. When he awoke, he heard a bubbling sound and saw an artesian spring flowing beside his lovely companion. *Where did this spring come from?* Drekel wondered.

He said to the flower, "What good is this?" and pointed to the water. "There are dozens of springs in the mountain." The flower seemed to nod in the direction of the spring's flow. Then Drekel understood. "Thank you little Troll Flower," he said and turned to follow the current of the bubbling waters. (No one had ever heard Drekel speak with gratitude.)

Drekel plunged through the dark corridors. Sometimes he had room to stretch his arms overhead, sometimes the passageway narrowed until he could only crawl, but he continued. He endured pain from sharp stones that lodged in his feet and bruised his knees. His hands and elbows bore new scrapes and developed deeper calluses. When he thought he could endure no more, he came to a crevice where sunlight blinded him as it spilled its brilliance upon the clear spring. Here the Troll Flower greeted him again! The secret way into the Tidendal Woods lay beyond!

•　　•　　•　　•　　•

Drekel's memories brought him back to the little flower as he touched her delicate pedals and understood that nature had heard his plea and led him once again to his Troll Flower. She had shown him the way out of the mountain and now she would show him the way to a permanent home in the forest.

"I have missed you," whispered an emotional Drekel. "You are my reason for knowing the beauty of the forest. You inspired me to leave the harsh world of endless night and escape to the land where beautiful flowers grow. When I was younger, the other trolls laughed and called me stupid, but I am the smart one who left that rocky mountain for the beauty of the forest. I will find where the spring flows in the forest, and I will keep it all to myself. It is my spring, my water and it will lead me to my home."

Drekel searched the forest for more signs of the bubbling spring. He tramped over many acres of land, always with his long nose pointing to the ground like a divining rod looking for water. He saw neither the animals of the forest nor the birds of the air, so intent was he on his quest. But they saw him.

"What is that crabby old troll looking for now?" asked a woodchuck. "Whooooo cares," replied an owl.

"As long as he's about his business, he's not bothering us. For that I'm cheerful," exclaimed a cheeky chipmunk. The woodlanders were atwitter with questions and speculations, but everyone avoided contact with the determined creature.

One muggy April afternoon, Drekel's search was suddenly interrupted by a horrific thunderstorm. He was deathly afraid of the jagged fingers of lightning and the loud BOOM of thunder. He still didn't understand the raging of nature even though he had experienced its authority in every one of his one hundred forest years.

Trolls have learned over thousands of years that their power is no match against the force of Mother Nature. Where do trolls get their power? It is general knowledge that mining trolls get their magical powers from the crystal rock hidden deep in the mountains. This is partially correct. However, there is more to acquiring magical power than mere physical properties.

Drekel had yet to learn this last fact. For now, he realized that over the last fifty years of his hundred forest years, his creative abilities had diminished to a few weak spells. When he first escaped from Lodespar Mountain, he could raise a pile of logs into the air or explode a tree stump with a twist of his long fingers. (He loved to perform these feats when he noticed a pair of woodland eyes watching him. To exhibit his power was a warning to the friendly creatures to stay away from him!) Now he could barely levitate a small branch.

53

"I wonder why my powers have grown so weak?" Drekel spoke to the huge fir tree he huddled under. He had begun to realize that there was more to troll magic than met the eye. "Drat this storm! Here I sit feeling sorry that I've lost my magical powers. Well, who needs those old tricks anyway! I just WANT to live alone. I WANT my own space and I WILL find that bubbly spring again and I WILL NOT share it with anyone. That is MY right. I don't NEED to share with any other creature. That old woodsman thinks he's hot stuff by helping the wood-landers. Well, I haven't seen him around lately. Maybe he got tired of helping others, too.

"All I did was work, work, work in the mines for crabby trolls who never appreciated me. All I did was mine silver, day after day after day. What's silver good for, anyway? One can't eat it. At least the forest pro-vides me with juicy berries, nuts and greens—things that have taste. In the mountain, all I ever ate was that awful pale gruel. Tasted little better than crushed rock!"

Fortunately, for the fir tree's sake, the storm abated and Drekel left his shelter. A sigh of relief emanated from the old tree. "That Drekel always complains. He gives me the creaks!"

The water-laden ground under Drekel's clumsy feet made looking for his elusive spring impossible. "How can I find my spring if there is soggy soil everywhere?" he muttered.

"Inner fortitude..." The east wind whispered.

"That's it!" he replied. Once it had helped him escape the mountain and now it would give him the strength to go on. He turned toward the northeast, noticing that the wind had dried this ground. Toward evening, he heard the faint, yet familiar sound of bubbling water. Tired as he was, he thought his mind was playing tricks on him. He took a few hesitant steps in the fading light and tripped. He fell smack in the middle of the bubbly spring.

"AT LAST!" He threw up his arms in jubilation. "I KNEW I COULD FIND IT!"

"We knew he could find it," echoed his faithful flowers.

Drekel followed the spring toward a beautiful heart-shaped pond. Across the spring, he saw the shadowy outlines of a little cottage and shed. Rage welled up in him. "I've come all this way," he wailed. "I've worked so hard to find my little spring. Now I find that someone has gotten here before me. What luck is this? What cruel fate!" In despair he staggered to the woods on the far side of the pond, slumped down under the closest tree, and wept. After hours of misery and self pity,

54

sleep mercifully took over.

For several days Drekel kept watch over the bubbling spring and its heart-shaped pond. He couldn't bring himself to leave "his" spring. Then he spotted a red-hatted elf walking between the shed and the cottage. As reason returned, Drekel remembered hearing the woodlanders discuss the cottage Alf had built beside a beautiful heart-shaped pond. *That must be the old woodsman's elf, but where is the big guy?* he wondered.

His question was answered a few day's later when a female gyrfalcon swooped into the clearing behind the shed. The red capped elf greeted her. Drekel crept closer.

Pung told Gerda Gyrfalcon that the woodsman had passed away and a farmer had taken Stig and Gotta away.

"I miss them, they were good company. The forest elves asked me to live with them, but I want to stay here in case Alf's brother comes from the land far away. Besides, I still need to look after the cottage. It's the least I can do for my master. Alf was my best friend," Pung said.

Well, so much for helping others, Drekel thought. *The old woodsman kicked the bucket from all the hard work he did for worthless critters. I'm glad I'm not like that!* He began to ponder, and the longer he pondered, the more strange thoughts came into his head. Suddenly he grinned his first grin in years, a grin so wide that it cracked his lips, a grin so enormous that several juniper berries fell from the bush on his nose. (They were used to his rages, but that smile was startling, even for a berry).

I've got it! he declared to himself. *That little Pung elf won't bother me. Why, he hardly bothers to come outside the cottage. And who knows when or if that woodsman's brother will ever show himself? Why should I give up my little spring. Why I don't even have to build a home. That wooden bridge with the drippy vines would suit me fine. The little red hat won't even know I'm there. And would you look at those berries, lovely tasty berries—right at my door step.* A few soft chuckles separated his thoughts. *This was meant to be after all.* The formerly distraught grumpy troll rubbed his long fingers together in glee.

That night, as the full moon was rising, the solitary mystical creature ambled toward the vine-laden bridge over the beautiful heart-shaped pond. Beside the bubbling spring, the welcoming Troll Flower blushed in the radiance of a moonbeam.

Chapter 7
Home

"W HO DARES DISTURB MY SLEEP?" the frightening troll demanded again as he surveyed the scene with a threatening frown.

What could two small frogs and a frisky otter do about a creature like this? Bertil stared at the horrific stranger. *Why he's half the height of a grown man.* (The otter remembered the men who worked at the tannery.) *And look at that nose.* Bertil blinked his eyes hard. *It's the longest one I've ever seen and could that possibly be a juniper bush growing on top?*

As movement returned to his body, Bertil, the diplomat, found his voice. "Sorry to disturb your sleep, sir. Lucia, Torv and I, didn't know anyone was living at the pond. We've been searching for a good home and then we saw this place—so clean and beautiful. We couldn't help but jump into the water and shout with joy! What, er, who are you, may I ask?"

"I AM DREKEL, THE TROLL," came the booming reply. "I don't care or want to know about your problems. I DON'T like critters around me. I want to live in peace, alone. This is MY pond. I was here first. LEAVE!"

"But, but, look at the size of us and look at the size of you. This pond is pretty large. Don't you think that it would be possible for all of us to live here?" Bertil eyed Drekel hopefully. "You live under the bridge and we, who are small and don't take up much room, could live anywhere else on the pond and not bother you."

"I know where I live." Drekel squinted his beady eyes in the bright sunlight. "And that is nowhere near where you are going to live. WHAT DON'T YOU UNDERSTAND? This is MY pond and MY pond only. I will NOT share it with anyone. GO AWAY, LEAVE, GOOD BYE!"

While Bertil tried to reason with Drekel, Torv climbed to Lucia's hiding place and huddled beside her. At last, rejected and dejected, Bertil swam over to them. "I tried to change his mind. What are we going to do now?"

"You gave it your best shot," Torv admitted. "He really is a mean, selfish, crabby creature. I would've been happy to live my whole life without ever meeting a troll if they're all like that one!

"What are you thinking, Lucia?" Torv turned to his little companion. "You've been awfully quiet. Don't be afraid of that grumpy troll. I can see right through him. Drekel is nothing more than a big old bully. Didn't Ragnar and Gabriella Beaver call the trolls bullies? This guy tries to scare us with his big, loud mouth. But just because he's louder and bigger doesn't mean he's smarter. Why, I'll bet the three of us are wiser than a whole clan of trolls!"

"Oh, Torv, you're funny and probably right." Lucia started to feel better. "But I'm not sure I want to put up with his attitude. I'm sad because we've found the perfect place for our new homes—plenty of pure water, lots of good food and excellent shelter. I just got my hopes up too soon, that's all. Let's see if we can find Pung." She gave Torv a little smile. "It's kind of funny. We came to cheer him up and now we need some cheering up ourselves."

The dejected trio glanced back at the moonflower-draped bridge and saw Drekel disappear beneath the foliage. Then they turned and started hopping and bouncing toward the little red cottage with white trim.

There was no sign of Pung at the cottage or the shed. But behind a large fenced area they saw a hairy four-legged animal with curved horns and sharp hoofs. "Oh, oh, another hairy creature. This being looks even more dangerous than our troll friend!" observed an agitated Torv.

They bolstered up their courage, agreeing that this creature might give them information regarding Pung's whereabouts. Bertil cautioned them to stay well back from the hairy one's head and feet.

Gotta, the goat, eyed the approaching trio with interest while she continued to munch on grass and a few green acorns. She had never seen a river otter carry frogs on its back. *They must have an interest-*

ing story to tell, she thought.

After the visitors introduced themselves, Lucia explained, "We have been traveling since early spring to find a new home. Along the way we heard about the woodsman and his elf, Pung. Then we heard that Alf had died and we thought that Pung might be lonely. We are orphans, too. We thought we could cheer him up with stories the wood-landers told us about his master."

Torv could no longer contain himself, "Then we saw this really great pond and thought, 'What a super place to live,' but," he pointed toward the bridge, "that grumpy, selfish troll told us to go away."

"We just want to find Pung," Bertil related, "and then we will leave. Do you know where he is?"

"Pung is having dinner at Farmer Johnsson's with Alf's brother Arne and his granddaughter Punzel. Pung stayed in the cottage after Alf died. Stig, Alf's horse, and I left to be cared for by Farmer Johnsson. You see, the farmer had to keep Alf's secret about Pung's existence. But after we left, Pung became more lonely. In the summer, Arne and Punzel arrived from Sweden, the same faraway land where Alf and Pung came from. Then Farmer Johnsson brought us back. Punzel and Arne have decided to stay for a while and Pung is ecstatic. We all like living by the beautiful heart-shaped pond."

By this time, Gotta decided that the otter and frogs were rather likeable and she should put a good hoof forward. "Pung has become very attached to Punzel and her grandfather," the goat continued. "Sometimes he accompanies them into town. He gets away with a lot because most humans can't see him. Only Alf, Arne, Punzel, the Johnssons and, of course, animals and forest creatures know of his existence. Why don't you sleep in the pasture with me tonight?" Gotta invited. "I usually sleep out nights in the warm weather. You can meet Pung in the morning. He's always the first one in the garden."

"Thank you for being so kind to us," Lucia replied. (She decided to trust this hairy creature.) "But maybe there's no reason for us to meet Pung if he isn't lonely any more."

"Nonsense!" snorted Gotta. "I'm sure that Pung would want to meet you. He'd like to hear that you admired the carvings Alf did for the woodlanders. Besides, Pung is clever. He may have an idea that would enable you to live by the pond despite that grumpy old troll."

Convinced by Gotta's logic, the weary travelers agreed to stay the night. In the embrace of the warm summer night, soothed by the starlit sky, anxieties drifted away and dreams of new homes near the bubbling spring of the heart-shaped pond emerged.

They awoke to the sight of a tall red hat bobbing through a sea of blossoms. The gardens and the pond were even more enticing in the morning sunlight. "I hope he likes us," whispered a wistful Lucia as she watched the little hat dart this way and that.

"Let's find out," suggested Gotta. The goat started toward the elf. "Mind you I have to be careful. Punzel doesn't like me in her gardens. Therefore, I will introduce you to Pung and leave. The rest is up to the four of you."

Gotta made good her word and returned to the pasture. Bertil warmed quickly to the chubby house elf. "You remind me of the forest elves I met this summer. They were dancing around a daisy ring. They said they were friends of yours."

"Yes, they are good friends. They wanted me to live with them after Alf passed away, but they like to live in the forest and serve nature and the woodlanders. I prefer to live in a house, or barn and serve humans and their animals."

"We came to visit you because we thought you might be lonely," Lucia confessed. "Now we understand that Alf's family has come to live with you and you have plenty of..."

Torv interrupted. "We heard about Alf from the woodlanders when Lucia admired the carvings he gave them. We've traveled for a zillion miles through the Tidendal Woods looking for a place to live and we're very tired. Can we stay here with you?"

"Ha, ha, ha," laughed Pung. "You sure are a spunky little fellow! What did you ask from me? A place to stay?"

"Please sir, elf." It was Bertil's turn to speak. "Torv is a bit impetuous. We've been searching for a new home with clean, pure water. This place is perfect but we're very disappointed that the troll won't let us live here."

"Oh, now I understand," Pung replied. "You've met Drekel. He thinks he owns the pond, but that's not true. The land of the Tidendal Woods, which includes the heart-shaped pond and the bubbling spring, now belongs to Alf's brother, Arne. Drekel's a good sort of troll. It's just that he's selfish and he's lost most of his magical pow-ers so he bellows, hoping to scare critters with his deep voice. Pretty effective, isn't it? He's trying to keep whatever he feels belongs to him away from everyone else."

Lucia liked the idea of charms. "Speaking of magical powers, how is it that Arne, Alf, the Johnssons, and Punzel can see you, but most humans cannot? That's what Gotta told us."

"They ate the honey that our bees made from the magical daisies that grew in a fairy ring. It started when Alf fell into a daisy ring and then later ate the magical honey. He shared some of the honey with his best friends, Farmer Johnsson and his wife. There was plenty of honey left when Punzel and Arne arrived. They ate it also. Whether one steps into a daisy ring or eats the magical honey, a human becomes endowed with the power to see magical creatures. Trolls, distant relatives to elves, are also invisible to humans. Punzel and Arne haven't had the opportunity to meet Drekel because he gener-ally sleeps during the day. That's one good thing about trolls. When my human friends and their troll tenant meet, WOW! That's an event I don't want to miss. Wait a minute!" Pung snapped his fingers. "I've got an idea."

"Oh, goody!" exclaimed Torv. "I hope it's a humdinger. Gotta said you were clever."

"Gotta, is pretty smart, herself," replied Pung. "Here's my idea. There's a nice piece of ground at the far end of the pond with hollow logs, stumps, tons of wild flowers, and pretty birch trees. Drekel rarely goes over there and then mostly at night. This place is hidden from the under side of the bridge by a little island with cattails. If you stay at your end of the pond, Drekel won't know you're there. This pond does have plenty of room for everyone."

"That's what I tried to tell Drekel but he wouldn't listen to me," explained Bertil.

Pung patted the otter's back. "Don't take it to heart, Bertil. His bark is far worse than his bite. Just look at him. Flowers won't grow where there's a mean spirit. Now come with me." Pung led them to the far side of the pond. Sure enough, everything was exactly as Pung had said. The trio were delighted!

Bertil claimed a cozy hollow log where flowering wood vines formed a lacy green and white camouflage for his home. His eyes immediately spied another good spot to build a slide into the wel-coming waters below. Lucia chose her home under the roots of a clump of birch trees, where she saw plenty of room for expansion—her mind already on entertaining. Torv found a ledge protected by tall grass and close to the water lilies. He wanted a convenient supply of boats for his yachting pleasures.

Home at last! The newcomers settled into an idyllic life style at the far edge of the heart-shaped pond. Bertil loved spending the waning days of summer frolicking in the pond's clear water. The elastic webbing between his toes enabled him to swim with great speed and dexterity and demonstrate his fishing skills. He would stay underwater for three to four minutes at a time catching crayfish, minnows, snails, bugs and clams. Lucia thought it fun to watch Bertil pry open clam shells with his paws. He gave her the prettiest shells to use for dishes. *I'm glad Bertil prefers the smaller food,* Lucia thought. *Some of the otters eat snakes and,* she shuddered remembering, *even frogs.*

Lucia enjoyed sorting through the many recipes collected from Gabriella and her woodlander friends. She made a list of ingredients for Bertil and Torv to gather before the long winter arrived. The daylight was already shorter and she wanted her home arranged and food supplies stored in plenty of time to relax in the cold weather days ahead.

Torv remained his carefree self. He enjoyed the view from his dwelling on the embankment. At first he kept a wary eye on the bridge, but as there was no commotion from that end, he soon lost interest and turned his attention to other interests. Occasionally Torv consented to gather food for Lucia, but he was most helpful as her culinary taster and adviser. Between snacks he enjoyed the abundant supply of lily pads and polished his sailing skills. When the air was too calm for sailing, he would bask in the sun and watch Bertil romp and slide down the steep sandy slope near his log home. Torv was fast becoming a very roly-poly green frog.

Punzel and Pung's digging, replanting, pruning and harvesting in the seven heart-shaped gardens was observed by the three new inhabitants. Lucia admired the flaxen-haired girl who worked diligently beside Pung. She also liked Punzel's way of dressing, particularly her garden aprons. Lucia wished she could have an apron too. *An apron would look very smart on me when I entertain,* she daydreamed.

Bertil's playful antics didn't go unnoticed by Punzel. Pung told her about the latest additions to the pond, but no mention was made of Drekel. Punzel liked to rest on the bridge and watch the playful otter cavort. He would skitter down his slide, flip and dive into the deeper water, swim back underwater, hop up to his slide and repeat this routine over and over again. *What a merry little fellow, with a lot of energy,* she thought. *I wish I had all of his energy to tackle these gardens.*

She looked for Lucia and Torv, but because of their small size, they were harder to find. Punzel finally did see Torv sailing on one of his lily pads. A frog sailing! She could hardly contain her surprise.

"This land is getting more curious all the time," she remarked to Pung and her grandfather at dinner as she told them about the little sailor. Pung smiled in his shy, knowing way. "Why, Pung, I believe you're still keeping secrets from me," accused Punzel. "You've not told me everything that's going on in this magical land, have you? I guess you want me to figure it out for myself. Okay," she sighed with determination, "I'll prove to you that I can. But first, I'm going to make Torv a sailor's hat. A cute, spunky frog should have a hat for wind protection."

Punzel looked over her quilt scraps and found enough pieces for several sailor hats. I don't think he would mind his hats matching our curtains or my bed cover, do you, Pung?" she chuckled. "This colorful fabric would suit him better than the traditional sailor's white. After all, he's a very special sailor. This is going to be fun!"

Pung watched the happy girl make a little hat pattern. *Those small pond creatures have brought a new light to Punzel's eyes, but will she be as happy when she learns who lives under the bridge?* Pung wondered.

Chapter 8
Surprises, Planned and Unplanned

Punzel tried to learn about her grandfather's activities in the shed from Pung, but the little elf proved to be as close-mouthed as Arne. *Okay,* she thought. *Secrets, secrets, and more secrets! Well, I can have secrets too.*

Punzel put on her thinking cap and came up with an idea. *I'm pretty good at knitting and Farfar really needs a warm sweater for winter.* (Punzel noticed that Alf's sweaters were a little short for her taller grandfather). On her next trip to New Hope, she bought many skeins of bright red and navy blue wool yarn, plus two skeins of white which she hid among the groceries. At home, she quickly unloaded the parcels and carried the yarn to the loft. *The soft blue and white yarns I'll make into a cozy sweater for Farfar, and the red matches Pung's hat. He needs a warm scarf and mittens. There will be plenty of time to finish my projects before Christmas. Won't Farfar and Pung be surprised?* She grinned with satisfaction.

That mood lasted but a few minutes until she remembered another important date. *Oh, no! I forgot Farfar's birthday is only three days before Christmas. It's not fair to give him one present for both occasions. A heavy wool shirt would be another good gift, but I don't think I'm skilled enough to sew a man's shirt. There's some nice warm shirts at the general store in New Hope, but I've spent all my money on yarn.* She pondered and twirled her braids for a moment. *Maybe I could earn the money to buy the shirt. When that nice, Gus larsson, brought more oats for Stig and Gotta last week, he said he was making bee's wax candles for extra money. Farmer*

63

Johnsson raises sheep on his farm and Mrs. Johnsson spins and dyes the wool and weaves it into beautiful rugs that Mr. Nelson sells in his store.

What can I make that people would like to buy? Punzel thought back to her life in Sweden and suddenly memories of Nordvik's pantry and her grandmother's gleaming jars of jams and jellies came to mind. *I'll make jams and jellies like Farmor did and ask Mr. Nelson if he will take them in trade for a woolen shirt. I'm sure they would sell in his general store.* Punzel's braids bounced in agreement. She put the last skein of yarn into the old steamer trunk. *Won't Far be glad to know we are doing so well in this new land? I must write to him this evening. I've not written as often as I promised and I have to tell him about the darling otter and frogs living by our beautiful heart-shaped pond.*

Once her yarn was safely hidden, Punzel made another decision. She would ride Stig. *He has a good nature to pull the wagon,* she thought, *but I bet he'd be happier without it. Stig and I can explore the Tidendal Woods to find more berries for my jams and jellies. The gardens only provide enough for our use. I'll need buckets and buckets of fruit if I'm to earn enough money to buy grandfather a new wool shirt.* She changed into her riding clothes, another adventure before her.

"Just you and I," Punzel said to Stig later as they entered the forest. The horse whinnied his approval. Horse and rider trotted under the vast green canopy as filtered sunlight spilled softly onto the forest floor. The only sound was their gentle breathing and the rhythmic thud of hoofs striding over the rich organic soil. The cool shelter from the lanky overhead branches provided relief from the last heat wave of summer.

The forest rewarded the quest of the twosome beyond Punzel's dreams. Plump juicy blackberries clustered on bowed spiny branches sprawled beneath the tall stands of oak, ash and wild cherry. Dainty blueberries graced the low moist areas and beckoned to the gatherers. "Come here, take us with you," they seemed to say. But this day her baskets were full. "I'll be back for you," she promised.

Punzel and Stig returned many times to the bountiful Tidendal woodland. Each trip was a treasure hunt, overflowing wicker baskets the reward. Their search led them to all parts of the vast forest. They felt the exuberance of the magnificent Norwegian Pines and the fragrance of their warm needles after a rain shower. Their eyes bathed in the splendor of the fall forest hardwoods as their wardrobe turned from green to shades of red, yellow and orange. And beneath the trees, they saw the emergence of the delectable fall mushrooms.

Pung was a great help as he faithfully worked in the seven heart-shaped gardens, giving Punzel the much needed time to gather and process her precious preserves. Pung kept Punzel's secret from Arne which wasn't difficult since Arne spent more and more time in what he now affectionally called "Alf's workshop," a section of the large shed. Arne became acquainted with Alf's woodworking books and was following in his brother's footsteps. *It's a shame to leave my bror's work unfinished,* he reflected as he practiced his carving skills. Arne, still the farmer, also noticed many tools that would come in handy for projects of his own. *It sure would be a good idea to rebuild the hen house and buy some chickens in the spring. Punzel would enjoy the convenience of having our own fresh eggs. By golly, I'm sounding more and more like my barnbarn. This land sure has its way.*

Mr. Nelson was impressed with Punzel's glistening jars of jams and jellies. She used some of her quilt pieces to fashion colorful covers for the lids and then secured the fabric with lengths of cotton ribbon she had brought from Sweden. Not only were the preserves well received, but Punzel's decoration, a reminder of their beloved homeland, was much admired by the Scandinavian village women. Punzel was soon able to purchase the wool shirt she wanted for her grandfather and there was enough money left over to buy a bag of his favorite licorice- flavored candy. Mr. Nelson told Punzel that he would be happy to sell more of her jams and jellies. *I have a way to earn money.* She danced with glee. *I am becoming more independent.*

•   •   •   •   •

The weather on the last days of September turned unpredictable. Mother nature had a hard time deciding whether she wanted the warm summer breezes to stay or invite the north wind to make an appearance. The inhabitants of the forest experienced several days of gentle warm winds, which encouraged the flowering plants to produce more buds. Then followed cool damp days of bone-chilling winds that turned beast and vegetation toward thoughts of hibernation. (Topsy turvy weather could only lead to trouble.)

This day started out like one of the warm, tranquil, summer ones. Lucia experimented with an oat cake recipe. Bertil gathered hazelnuts in hopes that the little cook would roast and caramelize them. Torv donned a yellow flowered sailor hat made by Punzel and boarded his favorite lily pad to take advantage of a light southerly breeze. He looked very natty since Pung had presented him with the hats. (Punzel was shy about intruding on the privacy of the pond folk.) When Torv sailed, he would wave to her if she was watching from the bridge. *Perfect,* he thought as he hoisted the sail and the golden maple leaf sail filled with air. He glanced toward the bridge to see if Punzel might be watching his little craft glide gracefully across the rippled water. She wasn't there so Torv, in his nonchalant manner, stretched out on his back to soak up the comforting sunshine.

Arne sawed logs for the cook stove and fireplace. Gotta munched away, as usual. Her eyes strayed occasionally to Arne, wondering why he worked so hard at such a senseless chore: hauling the dead trees from the forest, cutting the trees into small logs, stacking the logs, carrying the logs into the cottage, stacking the logs again, burning the logs, and finally carrying out the ashes left from the logs. It seemed much easier to grow a nice thick coat of hair and forego the work.

Pung sorted the wheat and oats Farmer Johnsson had given Arne. The elf selected the best sheaves of grain and put them aside to feed the birds during the winter. He was as thoughtful of the wild creatures as he was of Stig and Gotta.

Punzel astride Stig's back was deep in thought. She never ceased to marvel at the majesty of the Norwegian pines as they passed beneath the huge, needled branches. *These trees must have been here since the beginning of time.* Her attention turned toward Stig. *In his way, he is as majestic as those trees. There is so much strength in his body, yet he moves with such grace. I feel the power of his muscles yet he walks like we are floating above this forest carpet.* Not a whisper did she hear. It was as though the dark towering trees absorbed all foreign intrusion of sound and light. Suddenly they left the shadowy green world as the brilliant foliage of hardwoods replaced pine.

Mesmerized by the vibrant display, Punzel failed to notice the change in weather until a blast of cold wind blew down through an opening in the colorful leaf canopy and swirled falling leaves into a gigantic funnel that rose in Stig's path. An ordinary horse would have reared up on his hind legs in fright and bolted through the forest, leaving his rider to suffer the consequences of a bad fall. Not Stig. He snorted, nodded to Punzel, as if to say, "It's okay, I see it," walked around the swirling tower of leaves and continued homeward.

The changing weather also created unexpected events on the heart-shaped pond. The temperature dropped abruptly as the wind shifted from south to north and the pond became an agitated caldron of cross waves that caught Torv's lily pad and rolled it out of control. Then, that same swirling rogue wind from the forest repositioned itself above Torv and descended.

"I'll show you how to sail!" the wind seemed to roar. Torv's small body was no match for this threat. Sailor and craft were picked from their watery route and hurled like a falling star streaking across the sky. They crash-landed in a bramble bush by the side of the pond's wooden bridge. The disheveled frog lay underneath a ball of shredded debris that once had been his favorite boat. This time, the wind HAD raised havoc.

Seconds later, Torv's familiar screams pierced the air. "Somebody help me quick before that old troll gets me!"

Chapter 9
Maelstrom

What strange weather we're having today! Punzel's legs hugged Stig's broad back as she thought about the turbulent rogue wind. They emerged from the woods in time to hear Torv's shrill screams echo across the pond.

"Oh, no! Someone's in trouble! Hurry Stig!" She urged the faithful horse into a gallop. They arrived moments later to find the pond in turmoil. Bush and tree stood bare. Their once graceful limbs dangled, contorted and broken and their colorful remnants floated on the water's surface like pieces of a crazy guilt. Tattered lily pads, speared by loose twigs, huddled next to piles of spaghetti that were actually the remains of the spiky lance-shaped leaves of the cattails. Their velvety brown tops looked like firecrackers after a Fourth of July celebration. Above the fray, Torv's screams continued to blare like an air raid siren. Finally his worse fears were accomplished—he attracted the attention of the resident under the bridge!

"WHO DARES DISTURB MY SLEEP?" These bellowed deep-throated words, all too familiar to Torv, Bertil and Lucia, smothered Torv's wails. A long juniper-clad nose followed by a massive hairy head broke through a bedraggled mass of moonflower vines.

Punzel, startled by the booming voice, turned toward the bridge. The shock of seeing Drekel almost made her fall off Stig! She thought she was accustomed to this land of extraordinary sights, but this creature was beyond belief. Punzel surveyed the spectacle—long strange nose, coarse thick hair, large gnarled hands and feet, beady dark eyes and a knotted rope-like tail. Her conclusion: she had finally met some sort of . . . troll! She gasped. A troll living under their bridge! Her mind flashed back to the time when she picked the brambleberries to save for the pie she intended to bake for her grandfather's birthday. There were days when she was disappointed with the small amount of ripe berries. Punzel felt she might be closer to solving that puzzle. *How long has this creature been here and why are there blooming flowers in his hair? They, like the moonflowers were still blooming in this cooler weather. I knew those flowers had a secret!*

She glanced around and there was Pung and her grandfather, running from the shed. The tall one looked completely befuddled— mouth open, eyes unblinking. The short one displayed a look of dread on his usually cheerful chubby face. Another scream rang out and Punzel's eyes darted to the tallest brambleberry bush where she spied the small disheveled green body caught in the jumbled branches. She dismounted Stig and ran to rescue Torv despite her apprehension at the sight of the hairy creature watching her. Stig wanted to trot back to the pasture, not anxious to get involved with the beast who lived under the bridge. But he decided his mistress might have need of him.

Torv, although scratched and bruised, stopped screaming and relaxed once he felt the strong gentle fingers of the kind girl untangle him from his picky prison. He lay quietly in her soft hands while she tried to calm his shivering body.

Pung and Arne were soon beside Punzel, "I'm, I'm sorry, really sorry." The elf looked at the ground. "I couldn't think of a way to tell you about the troll. Then I figured it was best leaving your meeting to chance and, maybe, once you saw him you would sort of accept him. Please tell me I wasn't wrong." He shuffled his feet in the dry grass.

"I'm sure you did what you thought best." Punzel tried to ease the little fellow's conscience. "But it's a shock to see such a creature. Is he like the Norwegian mountain trolls I was told about in Sweden?" She shifted her braids with a toss of her head. "He looks somewhat like they described except for the juniper tree on his nose and those beautiful wildflowers in his hair. They're still blooming just like the moonflowers. I never knew mountain trolls grew flowers. I never knew trolls existed except in fairy tales. But they really do exist, don't they? I'm not imagining him?" Punzel finally ran out of steam.

"Yes, they really do exist." Pung looked at granddaughter and grandfather and was relieved to see that they were taking this discovery in stride. "Drekel, that's his name, is related to the Norwegian mountain trolls although he was born in the Tidendal Mountain. You're right, he's not like other trolls. Drekel has evolved into a woodland creature dedicated to the forest vegetation, but, as you can hear, he is still a troll, a very selfish troll. Alf and I had seen him wandering the forest, mostly at dusk or dawn. He doesn't mean any harm, we just left him alone as he's not in the habit of getting along with anyone else."

Torv wiggled in Punzel's warm hands, rapidly recovering from his fright. "Thank you," he said in a quivering, croaky voice as he looked up at his rescuer.

Punzel nearly dropped him! She could actually understand his croaks!

"He, said, 'thank you!'" Punzel turned to Arne. "Did you hear him?"

"Yes, Punzel, I did." Her equally surprised grandfather was still trying to take in Pung's story.

"What's happening to us?" Arne looked at Pung. "How can we understand frog talk?"

"Simple. It's a property of that water," The elf answered confidently while looking at the pond and its bubbling spring.

"Our water?" A very perplexed Punzel looked down at Pung. "What has our water got to do with talking frogs and we understanding them?"

"Well, it has everything to do with everything. Details are not my best side, but your bror knew the answer." Pung turned to Arne. "We can look through his writings after this predicament is straightened out. I don't know exactly where it's written, but I'm sure it's mentioned in his journal."

"CAN ANYONE HEAR ME?" shouted Drekel. (Trolls have an aversion to being ignored when they want attention.)

"ENOUGH OF THIS MUMBLY NONSENSE! I WANT EVERYONE TO GO AWAY. GO AWAY AT ONCE! THIS IS NOT YOUR POND. THIS IS MY POND! LEAVE. I WANT PEACE AND QUIET!"

"Just a minute." Arne needed to get a better understanding of this creature. "Before you continue shouting, my granddaughter and I

70

would like to know just who you think you are. It seems to me that you're the only one disturbing the peace and quiet."

"This is MY pond," grumbled Drekel. "I am Drekel, the troll. I was here first. That is MY spring flowing into this pond, therefore THIS IS MY POND."

"And just why do you think this is your spring?" Arne pointed toward the bubbling water.

"I discovered it in the rock beneath this forest." Drekel replied, "and I searched until I found where it came out of the ground. And there it is, MY spring. I can prove it! Look carefully at the ground beside the spring." Arne walked past the bridge and along the shore until he came to the bubbling spring.

"Now look under that rock." Drekel gloated, "Those are MY flowers. The Troll Flowers only grow by this spring. There is my proof! Who are you to challenge my ownership, anyway? Go! Leave me alone. I have already wasted enough time with you."

Arne stood admiring the dainty flowers. "I acknowledge your proof that this is the same spring you found in the forest underground. However, just because you find something does not give you the right to claim it for you and you alone. The Tidendal Woods and Lodespar Mountain are part of my brother's homestead, his land. What grew on this land belonged to him. Lucky for you, he wasn't a greedy, selfish person and he freely shared. To answer your question, he left this land to me and now I am the owner. You do not have the right to tell others what they can or can not do on my property. My granddaughter Punzel and I live in the little cottage and we also want peace and quiet."

"Please, Farfar may I say something?" (Punzel could hardly believe that she was about to talk to this creature). "I think I understand what Drekel is trying to tell us."

"You don't understand a thing about me!"

"I understand that you would like a quiet place in which to live and I believe this place suites you very well. I've seen Torv, Lucia and Bertil living here for several weeks. It seems, for the most part, as though everyone has enjoyed their own space, you included. This was an unfortunate accident caused by a mishap of nature, a freak wind." Punzel glanced fondly at Torv, still nestled in her hands. "Everyone was shaken by this incident and you certainly wouldn't blame a little frog for being frightened. He didn't intentionally disturb you. If you can't understand that, then maybe you don't belong here with the rest of us. That is your decision. My grandfather has made HIS position very clear."

Lucia and Bertil remained very quiet during the confrontation between the humans and the troll. They really admired the way Punzel and her grandfather had taken control of the Drekel situation and were relieved to see that Torv had survived his latest catastrophe. At least, they acknowledged, this mishap wasn't of Torv's own making.

Bertil and Lucia hopped over to the flaxen-haired girl. "We would like to say thank you, Punzel, for rescuing our friend Torv. We might never had been able to reach him without your help." The river otter bowed slightly.

"I can understand you too! Oh, my goodness. It's my pleasure, Bertil," replied Punzel. "Please excuse me. I'm still a bit overwhelmed with the knowledge that we can speak with each other. I feel that Farfar and I have come to a land of enchantment, like in a wonderful dream, and any moment I will wake up and it will all disappear. Let me give Torv back to your care," Punzel bent down and Torv hopped reluctantly from her hand. "He's quite a little trouper!"

"You don't know the half of it," chuckled Bertil.

"I would be pleased if you, your grandfather and Pung would come for lunch at my place before the weather gets too cold," invited Lucia. "We are most grateful to you."

"I'm sure we would enjoy that. Thank you!" Punzel was very pleased for a chance to get better acquainted.

"Well, Drekel," Arne turned a serious eye to the troll, "have you decided to live in peace with Bertil, Lucia and Torv as Punzel suggested or are you going to leave? It appears that everyone here is willing to share with you. Are you willing to stop fussing and share the pond with us?"

Drekel scowled. "I don't see why I have to share anything. I don't see why I can't live by myself. I need to think. This has upset my sleep. Everyone go away. I need to be alone." Drekel withdrew his head behind the ragged moonflower curtain and the remaining inhabitants of the heart-shaped pond departed for their homes with senti-

72

ments that they were glad that both storms were over. (However, no one thought this would be the last of them.)

•   •   •   •   •

Punzel, Arne and Pung sat at the trestle table with the pine tree carved in the end legs. Alf's journal lay open before them. Pung sat on a stack of books to give himself a better view. The researchers scanned through the later journal entries hoping to finding a reference to the bubbling spring or its pond. They found sketches of carving projects tucked between the pages similar to the designs Punzel had discovered in the tall bookcase. Pung was sure that hidden in Alf's fine handwriting was the secret to the magical properties of the spring's waters, so he encouraged them with every turn of the page. Several entries were of special interest to Punzel and her grandfather.

"June 10, 1897. I have received the pipe I ordered to bring the water from the bubbling spring to the cottage.

"June 12, 1897. It is hard work digging the water pipe into the ground, but I don't want the water to freeze in the winter.

"June 15, 1897. I have not made an entry until I could write that we finished. We now have water in our little cottage. The pitcher pump takes a strong hand to work, but it will ease as we use it. I am grateful for this wonderful water. It has given me rare knowledge of life and keeps me feeling like a young man. I feel deep kinship with those people from long ago."

"1897! That's only ten years ago!" exclaimed Punzel. "Alf carried water from the spring for almost thirty years! That was a lot of hard work!"

"Yes. I helped him." Pung pointed toward the latest entry. "That 'we' Alf refers to is he and me. Digging the pipe into the ground wasn't easy. We did a lot of hard work through the years, but it was well worth the effort and, as you know, Alf always had a good reason."

They searched a while longer, but the well-worn pages began to blur before their eyes. The exciting day had taken its toll on the inhabitants of the little red cottage beside the beautiful heart-shaped pond. Arne saw Punzel's eyes closing. "We need to get some rest. Tomorrow is another day. With fresh eyes, the search will be easier."

"Oh, Farfar, I want to keep looking. I can hardly wait to find out what gave the water its magical power." But then she yawned. "You're right, I really am tired, but I warn you, I will be up extra early tomorrow. God natt, Farfar. God natt, Pung."

That night, as Punzel, Arne and Pung slept the deep sleep of the

73

exhausted, Drekel was wide awake. He had a decision to make. Trolls are slow in processing their thoughts. The longer this process takes, the shorter their patience. The shorter their patience, the madder they become. The madder they become, the more frustrated they become. The more frustrated they become, the less sense they make, even to themselves, like the cat chasing its tail, going nowhere. The question of whether to share the use of HIS pond, HIS spring, HIS berries or leave HIS pond, HIS spring, HIS berries was one of the most difficult questions he had ever to answer.

Drat that man! Drekel stomped his large feet. *Someone is always interfering with MY life, MY quiet, MY peace. At least the old woodsman left me alone. This old man does nothing but stick his nose in MY business.*

The moon was threatening to leave the sky when Drekel realized he was, indeed, going nowhere.

"I'll SHOW HIM WHOSE LAND THIS IS. I'LL STAY! YES, THAT'S IT! I'll SHOW THEM ALL THAT I'M A STRONG, SIGNIFICANT TROLL!" he roared. The moonflowers quaked and shivered on their vines, the sturdy bridge creaked and moaned.

"If anyone gets in my way, I'LL USE MY GREAT POWERS ON THEM." Then he remembered his powers had diminished. "Anyway, I'll show them!" His decision made, Drekel calmed down and so did the bridge. The plant life surrounding them breathed a sigh of relief and nodded with pleasure. They certainly wanted the grumpy troll to stay.

At the far end of the pond Bertil, Torv and Lucia had been awakened by Drekel's clamor. Torv called out, "Lucia, Bertil, did you feel the ground shake?"

"I wondered if it was the ground or me." Lucia answered.

"Everything's okay," Bertil reassured them. "Drekel's just letting off some steam. Must be part of a troll's nature."

Torv was annoyed. "I wish he would take his nature and move it somewhere else."

As the troll's ranting diminished, Bertil turned over on his side muttering, "Drekel's finally worn himself out," and was soon fast asleep. Peace descended once more on all the inhabitants of the heart-shaped pond.

The next morning, Pung got milk for breakfast from the box over the little spring and noticed Drekel sitting near the pond's edge. Pung hastened back to the kitchen where Punzel was preparing breakfast.

"Punzel, Drekel is by the herb garden. He never comes this close to the cottage in the daylight. What do you suppose he is doing there?"

"Let's find out." Punzel put their breakfast aside. "Farfar is working in the shed. Maybe Drekel will talk to us since he's in our garden. Come on!" She grabbed her sweater and led Pung out the front door.

"Good morning, Drekel," they greeted the troll.

"Doesn't look like much of a good morning to me," came the reply. "Didn't get much done last night. Not much at all. However, after some, uh, concentration, I've come up with an answer for the old man."

Pung turned to leave. "Okay, I'll go get him."

"No, you won't!" retorted Drekel. "I want to talk to the girl. She can give him my answer.

"Here's the way I see it," he raised his large right hand toward Punzel. "If I want to live by MY pond, MY stream, MY bridge, MY flowers, MY berries, I have to allow those creatures to live there, too." He pointed one branch-like finger toward the far end of the pond. "That's what you said. Well . . . I want to stay. . . so they can stay, but they'd better not get in MY way. Tell THAT to the old man."

"I'm glad to hear you're becoming more reasonable." Punzel tried to be diplomatic. "You're a rather nice troll, I think, being you're the first troll I've met."(She also had to be honest.)

"None of that stuff. Just do as I say. Good bye!" Drekel disappeared into the bushes beside the bridge.

"Gracious, Pung, that troll's impatient. I guess we'd better tell Farfar that Drekel has decided to stay."

Breakfast was unusually quiet as the diners pondered the events of the previous day and the latest Drekel decision. Arne was the first to speak. "I think Drekel's made the right decision for all of us. We need to appreciate each other's differences and we need to learn tolerance for those differences we don't agree with. Drekel's come a long way in one night. He's trying to accept the concept of sharing, but he HAS to learn how to be comfortable with it and that's hard work. I'm sure he's never worked so hard for anything as he did to find the little spring. He didn't want to give that up so there's hope for the rest. We must be patient. I don't think peaceful co-existence will come easy to that one."

After breakfast Punzel opened the journal. "Farfar, listen!" Punzel reread an entry. "'I am grateful for this wonderful water, it has given me rare knowledge of life . . . I feel deep kinship with those people

75

from long ago.' We were so tired last night we missed the importance of what we read. Pung was right! Somewhere in his journal there is an explanation about the water's gift. And then, there is this reference to people from long ago."

"Ja, you are right, Punzel. We have missed something by being too anxious! Let's go back and watch for entries about ancient people as well."

"This is getting more and more curious. Farfar!"

The morning passed quickly as their eyes quietly scanned the pages and their minds floated in a sea of words. Finally Arne rubbed his forehead. "I need to get a little fresh air. My old eyes are starting to blur again."

"I could use a little sunshine myself, Farfar. Do you want to come with us, Pung?"

"No, thanks, Punzel. I want to read a bit longer. I feel we're getting close to the answer. I just wish I could remember more."

Punzel and her grandfather were scarcely out the front door when Pung's excited voice called, "Come back! Come back! I've found it!" Pung's round cheeks puffed out with excitement as the researchers gathered once more in front of the familiar journal. His chubby finger pointed to an important passage: "November 22, 1877. My suspicions are well founded. I've learned why I can communicate with animals."

Punzel and Arne stared at the words, hesitant, as the ink shimmered with the knowledge of a secret that would change their lives. Cautiously the old man, the young girl and the elf began.

"When you read what I have uncovered" the Journal said, "you will understand why I wanted you to visit this land, my dear bror. At first it was to share the freedom, peace and beauty of this wondrous land with you. But as you will also learn through my tale, there is much, much, more to life on my homestead."

All eyes turned to Arne as they finished this passage. He swallowed, visibly shaken, as though his brother Alf had reached across time and touched him. They exchanged smiles of understanding and then were irresistibly drawn back to the written page.

Chapter 10
The Legend

A rne, Punzel and Pung settled more comfortably in their seats as they began to read the life-changing odyssey in Alf's Journal.

"My tale begins when John Johnsson's mor asked John and me to help clean out her attic. The attic was filled with stacks of wooden boxes containing his farmor's books and keepsakes. Those wooden boxes were clumsy and heavy. I slipped on my third trip down the steep narrow stairway and the books and I went tumbling. As I placed the books back in the box, a small hand-bound volume caught my eye. It had an unusual cover of thin dark leather with bent corners and scuff marks that showed much use. The pages were of various quality and ranged in color from off white to tan. I wanted a better look so I set the little book aside and continued removing the rest of the boxes from the upper room.

"When John and I had finished our task, I handed him the book. 'I was drawn to this, John. I don't know why. Do you know anything about it?'

As John thumbed through the book, a big smile spread across his face. 'I had forgotten. This is farmor's favorite journal! Remember? My farmor liked history. She came to this country when she was an older woman. And since she didn't have the responsibility of young children she was able to spend a lot time searching for stories about her adopted land. She had become intrigued with the shape of your pond and eventually a friend located the history of it. After that, farmor told me to persuade you to move from Sweden. She remembered you as my boyhood friend who liked to carve and was convinced you should own the land with the heart-shaped pond. Take it, Alf.' He handed the book back to me. 'Farmor would want you to have it. I'm sure the history of your land is in there.'

"I brought the journal home and read as soon as my chores were finished. My hands trembled when I came across the story I was looking for. Mrs. Johnsson's friend, who worked in a Chicago library, found some interesting information about New Hope and its surrounding area in an obscure stack of records and sent it to her. This information spoke of a legend that records the history of a heart-shaped pond, its bubbling spring flowing from the nearby mountain, ancient trees, and wisdom that transcends the centuries.

"According to this legend, the people of the ancient world who lived on this land before recorded time were kind, gentle and industrious. The nearby mountain supplied the valley with clear, pure water that encouraged the abundant growth of wild berry bushes and trees bearing nuts and fruits. The stately Norwegian pines flourished as well as trees of ash, oak, beech, and birch. The people drank freely from the clear waters, learning what berries, vegetation, roots and seeds were good to eat and cultivate. They enjoyed watching the animals of the forest, and the birds of the sky, but they never captured or killed any creature or used any wood that hadn't already fallen. 'The animals, birds and trees are like us,' said the people. 'They too need to be free to bloom and grow.' The people worked hard for their survival and built simple tools to make their work easier. They made fire from the fallen wood for warmth and cooking and believed that some of the wood should be preserved for its beauty. Using their simple knives, they became expert woodcarvers. The forest animals and birds were their models. They deemed these carvings to be a tribute to nature for their prosperity in the fertile valley.

"For hundreds of years, this valley in the shadow of the mountain thrived. Then a drought came upon the land. The mountain's streams stopped flowing into the valley. The berry bushes stopped producing, the nut and fruit trees didn't have strength to make seed. The ferns, grasses and flowers couldn't grow. The people grew hungry and thirsty. There was barely a drop of water to be found. But the spirit of the people did not dry up. Despite their hardships, the people remained kind to the animals of the forest and the birds of the sky. 'These creatures have spirits as well,' the people said. And the creatures of the forest saw good in the people. 'What can we do to help them?' the owl asked the otter. 'What can we do to help them?' the squirrel asked the bear.

"Pondering this question, a clever fox named Eskil decided to motivate the other foxes. 'We're suppose to be clever and smart. We need to uphold are reputation and use our intelligence to help the inhabitants of this valley. Listen to me! The streams have always flowed from the mountain. It's reasonable to believe we must look there to find why they have stopped flowing.' The foxes thought this a good idea so they set off toward the mountain. In those days, the mountain was young, with sharp peaks and deep crevices. The Adventurers slipped and slid over that dangerous terrain. It wasn't long before their bodies and paws were covered with cuts and painful bruises and most of the foxes turned back in defeat. Eskil and four others dared to continue.

"Halfway up the mountain, they found a cave entrance and decided that if water was to be found, it was logical that it started deep within. Thus their journey into the mountain began through a narrow tunnel barely illuminated by streaks of daylight that squeezed through irregular slits in the rough rocky walls.

"Gradually, the foxes' vigor returned and their eyes grew accustomed to the cool, dim mountain world. Their renewed courage was, alas, to be short-lived. Around the next bend, the sounds of angry voices and loud thumping assailed them. They slowed their pace, as each step brought those sounds closer and closer, until before them loomed what appeared to be a huge mouth with long, sharp teeth. They had never seen such a sight in the forest! Their bodies shrank with fright as they stared at dozens of drippy stalactites hanging from a domed cavern ceiling and tall narrow stalagmites rising from the floor to meet them. Through this barrier deep-throated roars echoed off the distant walls and high craggy ceiling. Seven large, hairy creatures with long noses, small beady eyes and rope-like tails huddled around a blazing fire. Their heavy-lipped mouths opened to displayed sparse brown teeth as they yelled and pounded the floor with stout wooden clubs. Flames from the fire cast hostile shadows on the rough walls making the shadows appear to dance in and out of the gigantic teeth-like formations.

"Eskil's friends turned in horror and braced their hind legs for a hasty retreat. But Eskil stood before them and held up one paw. 'We have come too far to give up now,' he whispered. 'The good people of the forest are depending on us. These creatures must know why the streams don't flow. We will wait until they sleep and search the mountain for water.'

"The plan was accepted. But while they waited for the creatures to fall asleep, drowsiness overcame the foxes. Eskil was awakened by thunderous snoring. Even in slumber, the creatures made a lot of noise! He crept toward the sleeping hairy hulks to get a better look. The fire's glow illuminated mounds of sparkling stones— greens, blues, reds, yellows and violets—that formed colorful pillows for the hairy foreboding heads. Eskil decided it was safe to start their search. He crept back to wake up his friends, who immediately complained of cramped, stiff legs and empty stomachs. 'Maybe we can find something to eat.' He offered encouragement as he watched them stretch and crawl out of their hiding place.

"Preferring to leave the largest cavern to its sleeping occupants, they explored other caverns and caves that revealed more caches of sparkling jewels and huge sacks of oats and other grains. In one cavern they found small dried pears and apples, much more to their liking. They discovered several damp areas, but as they looked for larger signs of moisture, their answer was always the same: more rocks! Disappointed, they wound their way back through the maze of tunnels back to the sleeping creatures and hid to observe them. 'They must have water somewhere,' they reasoned.

"Eventually the mountain creatures awoke, grumbling, and jostled one another while they made breakfast in a large metal pot suspended over their rekindled fire. The pot produced a mushy soft grain they transferred into wooden bowls. The knobs on the ends of each creature's long three-fingered hands were used to scoop the mush into his trench-like mouth. They drank from smaller bowls filled by a tall vessel kept in a dark grotto across the chamber. Arguing and grumbling was kept to a minimum as they stuffed their mouths. Eventually the hairy creatures ate themselves full and reclined, falling into a slight stupor, their stomachs visibly satisfied.

"Eskil's interest in the tall vessel was stronger than his fear of being discovered. He decided this was a good opportunity to explore the grotto and motioned the other foxes to follow. They crept stealthily along the cavern walls, taking advantage of each shadow as snores emanated from the bulbous mounds.

"Three flat rocks rested under the moist water vessel. The foxes shivered with delight. 'There's lots of moisture on these rocks,' observed Eskil as he tugged at the closest one. 'Help me.' They tugged and pulled and pulled and tugged. Finally, the heavy rock gave way to expose a pool of cold pure refreshing water. One fox, unable to hold back his elation, plunged into the water, drinking his fill. The others followed, unaware that their movements had been discovered. Too late they noticed a large hairy creature bending over them, club in hand.

" 'Who goes here? Who is stealing our water? Speak!' came a deep-throated command.

" 'I am Eskil and these are my friends,' squeaked Eskil as he tried to control his shaky voice and limbs while keeping a eye on the menacing club. 'We are from the forest in the valley below. Please spare us. We mean you no harm. We were just, uh, a little thirsty, sir.'

" ' Spare us. We mean you no harm?' Echoed the creature. 'Ha, ha. You think a little fox like yourself could possibly hurt us?' The creature's dark, beady eyes surveyed the five sleek, dripping bodies. 'Although, looks to me like you WERE stealing OUR water. But . . . it isn't every day that woodlanders pay us a visit. Few are brave enough to enter the halls of the mountain trolls. I might spare your lives, for I am an honorable and reasonable troll, if you can give me a good reason for your entering our mountain. I guess our security isn't what it used to be.'

" 'The water from your mountain has stopped flowing into the valley,' explained Eskil. 'There's hardly water to drink or food to eat. The bushes can't grow berries, the trees don't bear fruit and the fern, grasses and flowers won't grow. The good people of our valley are getting weak. We have come to the mountain for help. You must know why the waters don't flow.'

" 'What if I do?' replied the troll. 'That is OUR business. This is OUR mountain, OUR water, and we do with it as we please. It pleases us to stop the flow of water out of our mountain.'

" 'Why?' Eskil was now more perplexed than frightened.

" 'Mining colored rocks is our life's work. Lately we've beat our clubs till we're near worn out only to find less and less of our pretties. We've stopped the flow of water because it might be washing away our treasures.' The large creature turned sad.

81

" 'If we can help, will you release the mountain's water?' Eskil had an inspiration.

" 'Ha, ha. How can little animals like you help big, powerful trolls like us?'

"Suddenly, it dawned on Eskil. 'How am I able to communicate with you? In our forest, only animals and birds can talk with one another.'

" 'I am Dangor, chief of this clan of mountain trolls. We are powerful magical creatures endowed with the ability to talk with all creatures of the land and sky. We choose to remain unseen and not speak with humans. Our ways our different. We have heard from other troll clans that humans ridicule and teach their children to be afraid of us. We will not communicate with such ignorant kind.'

" 'The good people who live in our forest don't think like those humans,' countered Eskil. 'These people respect all living creatures, yourself included. We'll prove to you that these humans are worthy of your kindness. If you are an honorable chief, you will give us the opportunity to help you and our valley,' stated the courageous and clever fox.

" 'Very well,' replied the troll chief, not wanting the foxes to think him less than just. 'I'll give you two days to come up with a solution. It you succeed, we will return the flowing water to the valley. If you fail, you shall return to the forest without water. I'm a fair troll.'

" 'Thank you!' Eskil was anxious to begin. 'We shall not fail.'

"Eskil held a meeting with his fox friends. 'While I was talking to Dangor, I thought of something that might help us. The humans adorn their knives, clothes and some of their eating vessels with a shiny, silver metal that is easy to bend. I know they find it in the rock below the forest floor. I'll bet that metal is in this mountain, too. The trolls have enough jewels. They could mine the silver metal and use it as the forest people do.'

" 'What a splendid idea! How do we find it, Eskil?'

" 'We need to make fire torches, hold the torches close to the walls and look for shiny rock. Those candles the trolls wear on their heads to mine jewels won't give off enough light to see silver veins.' The foxes searched high and low, up and down. Through the maze of winding tunnels they traveled, passing trolls, young and old who stared at the small furry strangers but offered no help. The forest creatures were unaware of the passage of time. For them day blended into night in this world devoid of sun and stars, where torch and fire light were their only balance. Dangor offered the foxes bowls of mushy soft grain. 'Ugh!' exclaimed one fox quietly to the others. 'I couldn't live on that every day, but at least he's trying to be nice.'

"The second evening, Eskil tripped over a discarded miner's club and his torch flared as it grazed the narrow passage wall. In the brilliant light, he noticed a zigzagged vein that looked like silver. He held the torch flame against the suspect rock to soften the ore, then used his sharp claws to scrape the vein. It was indeed the silver metal the forest people used. He hurried to tell the others.

"When Eskil showed Dangor the piece of silver, Dangor was not convinced. Eskil suggested that a troll put the piece on a rock resting in the hot fire. Soon the silver became malleable and Eskil taught the troll how to form it into a shiny jeweled ring. Dangor's eyes blazed with pleasure. Yes, this metal is almost as good as troll magic! Eskil then told the many ways the forest people used the metal and how it could benefit the trolls. Everyone cheered!

"Dangor pounded his club for attention! 'You have proven this beautiful and useful ore called silver can be mined in our mountain and we can make good use of it. You have fulfilled your promise to me and shown proof of your friendship with the forest people. Now I will show you that Dangor keeps his word. Perhaps I believe that your forest people are good. They are clever, and so are you, little fox. I shall reward you all and maybe some day every creature of the forest will think kindly of the mountain trolls. We have enough pretty stones. It is right to free the water.'

" 'How are you able to do that?' Eskil looked at the troll chief.

" 'I am the great and powerful Dangor. Come with me and I will show you.'

"Eskil and his fox friends followed Dangor to a cavern where the ceiling, walls and floor were encrusted with clear crystals. 'This is the heart of the mountain. Those crystals give all trolls born in this mountain the power to perform magical deeds. The only way we can use our power is by doing good deeds. If we use our power for bad deeds, we will lose it. Douse your candles and torches. Enter, please!'

"Then Dangor announced. 'You, Eskil, aren't the only one with ideas. Listen. I, Dangor the First, Chief of the mountain trolls, hereby, from this day forward, declare this mountain to be called Lodespar commemorating the veins of silver that flow through its rock. Now, watch the power of the mountain speak through my words.'

" 'Oh, mighty Lodespar hear my will. Let the waters flow forth from your depths and replenish the valley below. Grant special favor to the good animals, birds and people who live within this land. May they reap the bounty of your special water.'

"The cavern's crystals began to glow. Their color turned a translucent blue, the blue of a high sky on a cloudless day, then gradually changed to a luminous blue-green, the green of the warmest sea. The inner moun-  tain began to shake and the tremors reached far into the valley, where startled inhabitants rushed to their shelters and huddled in fear. Huge boulders spewed from the mountain and rolled into the valley where no boulders had been before. The mountain moaned as the gurgling started. Then came a rumbling sound as the headwaters of Lodespar Mountain cascaded downward, gathered force, and plummeted into the valley creating a vibrant river that cut its way across the dry forest floor. Other streams, brooks and springs spurted from the mountain's pores and formed ponds, lakes and tributaries.

"One tremor sent waves of water through the crystal cavern to form the headwaters of a precious spring that gushed through fissures in the massive mountain rock and swept under the forest floor spawning seeds of the Troll Flower as it flowed. The little spring emerged into the light of day, bubbled from its earthen channel and spilled into a meadow at the edge of the forest people's village. The mountain crystals had created magical artistry, an artistry akin to the figures carved by the finest woodcarver.

"When the tremors stopped, the forest inhabitants ventured from their shelters. The animals and birds saw the dazzling wide river coursing through the forest and the many waterways of streams, ponds and lakes. The good people saw the product of the crystal's artistry—a shimmering heart-shaped pond had been carved where their meadow had once been. And when the people, birds and animals drank from the heart-shaped pond, they discovered that the lovely pure water contained more than the sustenance of life. The water united them with the gift of understandable speech. Dangor had kept his promise.

"The passage of time brought greater unity to the inhabitants of the land in the shadow of Lodespar Mountain. The enduring river flowed faithfully from its mountain source and earned the name of Tiden River, or timeless river, and the woodlanders paid homage to the river for it's continual nourishment and named the valley Tidendal, the timeless valley.

"I write this day with the knowledge that providence has brought me to the Tidendal Valley, my land, home of my kindred spirits, the woodcarvers of ancient history. I am forever in debt to Mrs. Johnsson for bringing me to my destiny."

Chapter 11
A Piece of the Puzzle

Grandfather and granddaughter raised their eyes from the journal and looked at one another. They were destined to follow in Alf's footsteps. According to the legend, good forest people who drink the wondrous waters of the heart-shaped pond would receive the gift of understandable language between themselves and the animals and birds of the Tidendal Woods. Arne and Punzel had drank and understood. They were now the guardians of this land.

Punzel's mind whirled as she hurried through her cleaning chores. *We can see and talk with a house elf and a troll and communicate with woodland animals. Goodness knows what else we'll be able to do.* Punzel glanced at the calendar, October 3, 1907. She didn't think anything significant about the date and got out her sewing supplies. "Winter will be here before long," she remarked to her Grandfather, who sat at the little table whittling on a whistle.

"Ja, winter is just around the corner. I felt a cold nip to the air when I fed Stig and Gotta this morning."

"Oh, no! My flowers!" Her chores and quilt forgotten, Punzel dashed outside to see that Jack Frost had gotten there first. She saw that her hardy colorful blossoms had been painted white.

Arne tried to change the mood of his dejected granddaughter by suggesting that she take Stig for a ride to Lodespar Mountain. "Don't worry. Your plants will come up again in the spring. This afternoon looks to be nice and a trip will do you both good."

"Perhaps you're right." She put away her sewing. "A trip through the woods would be good for Stig." Her quilt could wait a while longer. Soon she had packed a cheese sandwich and a cookie for herself and an apple to share with Stig.

As usual, Farfar had a good idea, Punzel mused as she trotted Stig through the light, open forest. Her mood brightened with the sound of Stig's hoofs crunching the crisp leaves. *A few days ago there was a mass of colorful leaves on the trees and now they're on the forest floor.*

•   •   •   •   •

October 3, 1907 was Punzel's seventeenth birthday. Arne and Pung had been working on special presents—a bed and a side table to match Pung's furniture. That was the second reason Arne sent Punzel away from the little red cottage. They needed time to carry the new pieces from Alf's workshop and assemble the bed in the snug loft.

"Pung, I'm sure not getting any younger," Arne huffed as the tall and short woodworkers struggled to get the bed's heavy posts and headboard up the loft's narrow ladder. Finally bed and table were in place, but not without mishap, Arne bumped his head several times on the low slanted ceiling as they assembled the bed. "Up here, you have a definite height advantage, Pung. This is no place for a tall man!"

Down at the heart-shaped pond, other birthday surprises were planned. Pung had told Bertil, Torv and Lucia about the reason for the new furniture and they wanted to share in the celebration, too. Drekel remained aloof. Everyone wanted to give Punzel something that was particular to themselves. Bertil gathered several baskets of hazelnuts that Lucia caramelized. Lucia made a huge pot of Ansa Duck's soup. Torv gathered tall dried grass from the little pond's island and hauled it ashore on a train of lily pads. Then he braided the grass into a heart shape. Pung was delighted with Torv's talent and found an extra piece of Swedish ribbon, which Pung tied to the dainty grass heart. Torv was ecstatic. He was sure that Punzel would like his gift the best. They could hardly wait for the festivities to begin.

•   •   •   •   •

Punzel and Stig stopped for an early lunch on the bank of the Tiden River. "This cool weather makes me hungry." Punzel practically inhaled her sandwich and cookie. While Stig happily munched grass, she discovered some well-preserved dry grass with feathery tassels on the shore of the fast flowing water. *These would be pretty in a bouquet*, she fancied as she gathered and stored them in her saddle bag. They shared the apple and had started alongside the river in the direction of Lodespar Mountain, when Punzel saw Stig's ears twitch.

"What's the matter, Stig?"

"I heard a chopping sound in the distance," came the reply.

"Oh, my goodness!" Punzel nearly fell off her saddle. "Stig, did you answer me?"

"Of course," the horse replied. "I can talk as well as you."

"Then why haven't you talked to me before?" exclaimed the startled girl.

"You've never asked me a question that I needed to answer." The horse turned his head to look at the girl. "I did what you told me to do. That didn't require conversation."

"Can I talk with Gotta also?" Punzel asked.

"Of course. We all drink from the waters of the bubbling spring."

"Does Farfar, er, Grandfather know? Forgive me for stuttering," Punzel apologized. "I still haven't gotten use to the idea of talking with you."

"Yes, your grandfather figured it out after you heard those creatures in the pond talk and Pung found the history of the bubbling waters in Alf's journal. He told Gotta and me you would discover we could converse with you 'in due time,' whatever that means."

"Grandfather is very smart. He knows I've been distracted by the recent happenings and I've needed time to sort it all out. I'll be truly grown up when I understand the meaning of Tidendal's magic. Oh, Stig, I got so excited about being able to talk with you that I completely forgot about the noise you heard. Where did it come from?"

"It came from the south. Would you like to ride in that direction?"

"Yes. It could be some woodlander in trouble."

They turned and traveled south for quite a distance, stopping often to listen. As they drew closer to the disturbance, Punzel remarked, "I never realized how far sound could travel in the forest when there are no leaves on the trees. At last, through the bare branches they saw two men. One was swinging an ax.

"Stop, Stig," Punzel whispered, tightening his reins. Sensing Punzel's anxiety, Stig stepped back into the forest shadows. Patiently the horse and rider waited and watched. *They look like lumbermen,* she thought. *What would they be doing on Alf's property?*

One man pointed to a tree and the other used his ax to make a notch in it. Finally the one pointing took a map from a bag and made some marks on it while the other slung the ax over his shoulder. Apparently their work was finished, for a few minutes later they walked toward the river.

"They must be leaving," Stig noted. "What do you want to do?"

"After those men are out of sight, let's look around and see what they were up to." Punzel dismounted and proceeded toward the trees were the men had stood. As she moved closer, Punzel saw the gashes on the giant ash, oak, and maple. Each of the older trees bore a scar, each had felt a blow from the woodsman's ax. "Why are they hurting these wonderful old trees?" asked a tearful Punzel. "We must tell Grandfather!"

The cool wind hit their unprotected faces as Stig set his pace. Nostrils flaring, great puffs of crystallized clouds formed as his breath blew ahead of his strides. They reached home in record time. Arne wasn't in the pasture, he wasn't chopping wood, nor was he in Alf's workshop. Leaping from Stig's back, Punzel led Stig into the shed, removed the saddle and threw a blanket over him. She would come back, after he had cooled down, and give him water. No matter what her situation, she never forgot to take care of the beloved horse. Then she hurried toward the cottage's backdoor yelling, "Farfar! Farfar, where are you?"

"SURPRISE!" The cheerful voices of Arne, Pung, Bertil, Lucia and Torv greeted her as the back door of the cottage flew open and Punzel rushed headlong into a celebration.

"What are you all up to?" The astonished girl brushed her braids back and rubbed her cold hands.

"Happy birthday to you, happy birthday to you, happy birthday dear Punzel, happy birthday to you." They sang with heart, if not in tune.

"Gracious, I completely forgot what day it is! What a wonderful surprise. I can't believe you did all this for me." Her cheeks, already pink from the cold ride, glowed even more as she looked around the cheery room. The trestle table had been set with large, small, and tiny bowls and plates. In the middle of the table was a fancy cake with swirls of whipped cream frosting and by its side lay a large wooden tray of caramelized hazelnuts. A pot of steaming soup took center stage on the stove. As Punzel walked toward the festive table, she noticed a delicate grass heart by one plate. "Is this for me?" She shyly picked up the present.

"Of course, it's for you. I made it myself." Torv hopped along the table's bench and puffed up his chest.

"Thank you, Torv. It's quite the sweetest heart I've ever seen," praised Punzel.

"I told you that she would like it," Torv boasted to his friends.

"Everything is yummy!" The birthday girl was touched by the preparation that had gone into the special food. She requested the recipe for Ansa Duck's soup and told Bertil that she would help pick hazelnuts and learn how to caramelize them. Pung got compliments from all as they licked their lips over his mouth-watering cake. He explained how he had hurried to bake and frost it that very morning.

During the party Pung noticed a shadow outside the front window. He peeked out the front door, but saw no one. As he turned to close the door, his hat brushed against something. He looked up and saw a wreath of fresh, soft colored flowers hanging on a nail. He brought the wreath to Punzel. "This must be for you."

Punzel gently caressed the daisies, violets, and pansies tied together with vines. "Who could have brought these lovely fresh flowers?" She thought of her cold, frosted ones. "There are no fresh flowers in the garden."

After a long pause, Arne spoke. "Uh, hummm. There is one who has blooms."

"That old troll!" Torv croaked with satisfaction. "Well, what do ya know? Maybe he does have something good in him after all."

"I think we'll be seeing more of his good side." Punzel winked at her grandfather. "It's just a matter of time."

"And now, Punzel, you need to show everyone that quilt you've been working on. Please go to the loft and bring it down." Arne and Pung exchanged knowing looks.

"Farfar, I'm only half way through piecing the top. No one would be interested in seeing it like that."

"Oh, come on, Punzel. We want to see it!" Bertil coaxed. He could hardly wait to see Punzel's expression when she saw her biggest surprise.

Punzel finally agreed to get the quilt, but as she climbed the ladder she almost lost her footing when she saw the posted bed. "Farfar and Pung, I knew you two were up to something! How did you manage to get this awesome bed up here?" She scrambled to the top of the ladder and over to her new bed. Each post had an elf's hat carved

90

into its top and in the center of the headboard were sprays of forget-me-nots with a heart carved in the center. Next to the bed stood a matching table. On it sat a wooden horse candle holder and a ribbon-tied bundle of beeswax candles.

"You're all pretty sneaky." Punzel smiled through happy tears as she descended from the loft. "You didn't want to see my pieced quilt. You wanted me to see the beautiful furniture."

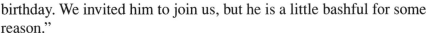

"The horse candleholder was an unfinished carving of Alf's." Her grandfather proudly admitted. "I tried to finish it the way he would have. And the candles were made by Gus Larsson. He wanted you to have a gift from him for your birthday. We invited him to join us, but he is a little bashful for some reason."

"What a nice thought." Punzel still blushed at the mention of Gus's name. "I'll be sure to thank him. Thank you all very much. You have made this one of the happiest days of my life."

Everyone agreed that it had been a special day. Before they left Punzel was toasted with a glass of lingonberry juice that reminded all of the warm days of summer.

That evening, Pung volunteered to bed down Stig and Gotta. Punzel and her grandfather relaxed and talked about the day's events. "I have to find a way to tell Drekel how happy I was to get the beautiful flowers. This land has brought many wonders to us, Farfar.

"Oh, the land! I forgot to tell you what Stig and I saw today. And besides that, I know Stig can talk!" Words started to tumble out of Punzel's mouth. "I was so surprised to see all of my friends and then had such a good time at my party that I forgot why I was in such a hurry to get back this afternoon." She took a deep breath. "Stig and I saw two lumbermen in the southern part of your woods. One had an ax and made a gash in the bark of the giant trees and the other wrote on a map. Why did that man hurt those beautiful old trees? Who were those men, Farfar?"

"I don't know Punzel. Don't fret! We'll go to New Hope tomorrow and visit Karl Lundquist. An attorney should be able to find the answers to your questions. I'm glad you and Stig only observed those men. They could be dangerous."

•   •   •   •   •

The morning sky was filled with gray, ominous clouds that matched Punzel's mood. "I can't help but worry about those men I saw in the woods yesterday, Farfar."

"It won't be long and you'll be able to tell Mr. Lundquist about them." Arne pulled on the reins to slow Stig down as their wagon approached the village.

Karl Lundquist was in his office and he was not happy either. "Come in. Come in. I'm glad you're here. I was just trying to arrange my schedule so that I could pay you a visit. Please, sit down.

"I have received some unsettling news." The kind attorney was decidedly agitated. "A document, that appears to be genuine, was delivered yesterday afternoon by two lumbermen."

Chapter 12
Out of the Past

A thin layer of ice covered the shore of the heart-shaped pond as the snow-covered landscape awoke to another fall day in the Tidendal Woods. The temperature inside the little red cottage was warm and cozy, but the occupants were heavy of heart. "These stitches don't look even." Punzel was attempting to finish her quilt. "I can't concentrate on my sewing, Pung. My thoughts keep going back to our visit with Mr. Lundquist. I've been trying to understand how those lumbermen could have gotten Alf to sign an agreement that gave them the right to cut down those magnificent old trees."

The chubby fellow added another log to the fire. "I remember Alf was upset when he was told by frightened woodlanders that there had been men in our forest. A few days later two men came upon us in the woods and told Alf they were working on nearby property cutting down trees to sell to sawmills for lumber. They thought his trees were good for lumber, also. But don't worry. I'm sure Alf never signed any papers giving those men the right to his trees."

"But it's been three weeks since Farfar and I went to the attorney's office. He has confirmed that the men Stig and I saw in the woods marking the trees with the ax were the same men who visited Alf this spring. What can be taking so long? Mr. Lundquist has had plenty of time to prove that Alf didn't sign the lumbermen's contract. Everyone knows Alf loved the woods. He carved only in dead wood and built his cottage from fallen trees. I can't believe he would let anyone destroy living trees.

"I've got to get out of the cottage for a while, Pung." Punzel folded her quilt and laid it on the bench. "I saw Farfar on the bridge. I'm going to see what he's doing."

Arne had found relief from his worries by watching the always energetic Bertil slipping and sliding down the snowy pond bank and tumbling head over tail into the icy water. "That is one way to keep warm." Arne motioned toward Bertil as Punzel approached the bridge.

"Bertil certainly is frisky, no matter what the weather," observed Punzel. "He acts like he doesn't have a care in the world. And I'm the opposite. I can't seem to concentrate on anything other than those lumbermen. We are supposed to protect the trees and the woodlanders who need the trees. I feel like we've let them both down because we can't defend them."

"There is some hope. I just got a note from Mr. lundquist. The judge has issued an injunction to stop the lumbermen from removing the trees until the hearing on December 20. It seems like a long time to wait for a settlement. If only they didn't have a contract with Alf's signature on it. I'm sure Alf didn't sign that paper. A clever person could copy Alf's writing but how do we prove it?"

"I think the lumbermen didn't expect anyone to arrive so quickly to settle Alf's estate." Punzel looked at her grandfather with love and pride. "They obviously didn't know about you and what a good, strong person you are to defend your brother's land. If only we could find a way to get those awful lumbermen to admit they did wrong."

In the cool still air, the worried voices of Arne and Punzel drifted downward to Drekel and gave him much to think about. His thoughts wandered back to the springtime when he was still in his cave by Lodespar Mountain and the commotion he heard as he left his cave for the last time. He had thought all the noise makers were his troll relatives, but those last noises came from excited woodlanders telling Alf something that disturbed him. Later when Drekel camped in the woods searching for his spring, he remembered seeing two men in the woods with Alf. One man took papers from a bag he carried and showed them to Alf. Alf looked upset, pushed the papers back into the man's hand and told the them to go away. Drekel remembered thinking, *now that's the kind of attitude I like! That old woodsman has spunk!* Drekel didn't understand what the strange men where doing in HIS woods but now that he had heard the conversation between Arne and Punzel, he realized that those men he saw in the spring must be the same men that Punzel and her grandfather were talking about.

Many days passed with only one thing on Drekel's mind. *Those lumbermen will destroy MY forest. I have to think of a way to keep them away from MY trees.* Drekel pondered, speculated, contemplated, cogitated and brooded. Trolls have a slow thinking process, but when their thoughts are sorted out, they are stubborn and stick to their decision, no matter what. *Someone must get those sneaky men to confess to writing the old woodsman's name on that paper. Who could be that clever?*

"ME!" Drekel shouted. "I AM THAT SOMEONE!"

Oh, no, contemplated Torv, all snug in his snow-covered home. *There goes that old troll again. I wonder what he's up to this time?*

Oh, dear, worried Lucia while frying some huckleberry fritters. *Are we in for another storm?*

Ha, ha, mused Bertil. *Maybe this fall won't be so quiet after all!*

Arne and Pung didn't hear Drekel. They were in Alf's workshop, sawing and hammering a Christmas present for Punzel. The only time they could work in secret was when Punzel took Stig for a ride in the woods.

Punzel and Stig were exploring Butternut Hill, a pretty little knoll near the south end of the Tiden River. They were well out of hearing range from Alf's workshop or the heart-shaped pond.

"This would be a lovely place to bring Farfar and Pung for a picnic in the spring." Punzel's hands shielded her eyes from the sunlight's reflection on the river while Stig discovered winter-green under the snow. "It would be nice to sit on this little hill and watch the Tiden flow merrily on its way. I feel guilty enjoying this peace while Farfar and Mr. Lundquist are trying to find a way to stop those lumbermen."

"Don't fret, Punzel. Your grandfather and Mr. Lundquist will outsmart those crooks." Stig nuzzled Punzel's shoulder.

They walked down to the river's edge. Punzel noticed that ice was forming close to the shore where the water was the calmest. Suddenly her thoughts were interrupted by shouts followed by three woodland elves running toward them. "Hello, Punzel and Stig. I'm Enok and this is Helga and Helmer." Enok motioned to his two companions and pointed upstream while trying to catch his breath. "There are two young trolls caught in the river's rapids."

"Please, can you try and help them?" asked Helga.

"We've tried to locate Gunvald Moose, but he isn't in this part of the woods," Helmer added.

"The trolls were jumping on those icy rocks above the rapids and they slipped and fell into the water," explained Enok. "We are too small to rescue them. Stig is big and strong. Could you try to get them out of the water?"

"We'll try," answered the horse. With Punzel on his back, they trotted toward the rapids, leaving the elves to rest. As they arrived at the top of the hill overlooking the rocky, churning water, they spotted the thrashing arms and legs of the trolls trying to catch hold of a slippery rock or grab a tangled tree limb. "They're certainly in a predicament!" She could also see that Stig and herself would be in danger of being swept along with the rushing waters through the maze of sharp rocks.

Stig approached the swirling water and took a few cautious steps. His hoofs slipped on the icy shoreline pebbles causing his ankles to strike against the larger rocks. Punzel was nervous and sat very still in her saddle, letting Stig concentrate on navigating into the river's swift current. As he edged closer to the struggling trolls, Gerda flew overhead and circled calling directions to Stig and giving words of encouragement to all.

The woodland elves arrived and watched from the shore as Stig approached the terrified, young creatures. "Steady, Stig. I think I can reach them now." Punzel carefully bent down from the saddle and grabbed one shivering body at a time. Gently she tucked the first troll behind her on Stig's broad back and then reached for the last water-soaked body, which she carefully placed on the saddle in front of her. When they were safely in place, she told Stig he could make his way back to shore.

The shore was alive with the sound of elves clapping and jumping up and down. They gathered moss to wrap around the shivering frightened little trolls as Stig came up the river bank. "Where do we take them?" Punzel asked the elves and Gerda.

"I saw two older trolls coming this way. They'll be here shortly." Gerda answered. I'm glad you were close by as Gunvald is at Blueberry Creek helping the muskrats. But even if he were here I doubt if he could have gotten these small trolls to shore without a lot of difficulty. You two make a good team. It's a pleasure to meet you."

"Thank you, Gerda. I was afraid we might not be able to help, but Stig is a real trouper. I'm happy to make your acquaintance also.

Pung has told grandfather and I that you are a heroine yourself."

"Here come the adult trolls!" interrupted the elves. Gerda, not being one to waste time flew off, after seeing that all was well.

"Pa!" screamed little trolls as they ran to grab the tail of the tallest troll.

The older troll bent down and patted their heads as they snuggled against his massive, hairy body. "What trouble have you two gotten yourselves into this time? Your mother told you not to leave the mountain."

"We didn't mean to get into any trouble," said one shivering little body. "We just took a teeny weeny step on one rock and we slid right into that mean old river." said the other.

"Sig and Punzel saved their lives," explained Enok.

"We were very glad that they were close by," said Helga.

"They are very strong and brave creatures," Helmer added.

"It seems we owe you a debt of gratitude." The tallest troll turned his attention to the rescuers. "I'm Dangor, The Forty-Third, chief of the mighty Lodespar trolls."

"Oh!" Punzel drew in a sharp breath. "Then it's true! The legend, I mean. Farfar, Pung and I were reading in Alf's journal about the trolls that lived in the mountain a long time ago and their leader's name was Dangor. You must be related to him." (Punzel saw a resemblance to another troll as well.)

"Yes, I am of his blood. Each of our leaders is named after Dangor the First, the chieftain who named Lodespar Mountain. In Dangor the First's time, there were good humans living on this land. We've heard that once again there are good humans living here. You must be one of them. Trolls have many powers, but we can't see what happens behind our backs. We of the mountain welcome you and are forever in your debt for rescuing our young ones. I must get them back to their mother. Ha, ha, she will make them warm in a hurry. We leave you for now, but you'll not be forgotten."

"I'm pleased to have met you, Chief Dangor, The Forty Third." Punzel curtsied and watched the four hairy creatures amble toward their mountain home.

"My gracious!" the amazed girl turned to the woodland elves. "They're quite well-mannered. They sure don't act like Drekel, but they certainly are as hairy. I can't wait to tell Farfar."

Enok couldn't help but laugh. "What you just saw is not what you always get. That's not the way they usually behave. Dangor was on his best behavior because he was impressed with your bravery. The Dangor leaders feel it is their duty to be polite when they meet someone they feel is worthy. Otherwise, they can be very rambunctious.

"Well, we should be on our way," Enok helped Helga and Helmer pick up a basket they dropped when they saw the little trolls in trouble. "We know you are anxious to get back to your cottage and we must get back to our homes as well. We're glad to have met you, Punzel. Travel safely."

"It was my pleasure to make your acquaintance also. Pung speaks fondly of you. Please stop by the cottage when you are near the heart-shaped pond. I want to introduce you to my grandfather."

On their homeward journey, Punzel confided in Stig. "Telling our adventure to Farfar will be just the thing to take his mind off of the lumbermen. I can hardly wait to see Farfar's face when I tell him we've met the descendent of the first mountain troll chief, Gerda and three of the woodland elves.

When they arrived home, Arne also had news. Mrs. Johnsson had stopped by and invited Arne and Punzel to their farm for a traditional Thanksgiving Day dinner on the last Thursday in November. She told Arne that he and Punzel needed to experience a custom that was part of their new life in America. Mrs. Johnsson had also invited another neighbor family to their dinner. They were the Erickssens, a newly arrived Norwegian family with two daughters. Gunilla, the oldest, was the same age as Punzel.

Grandfather and granddaughter sat by their cozy fireplace as they traded stories. "We couldn't have more diverse subjects, Farfar— Mrs. Johnsson, trolls and elves." Laughter warmed their spirits and, for the moment, troubles were forgotten.

Punzel could hardly wait for next Thursday. She would be meeting a girl her own age and there would be a chance for a new friendship.

Chapter 13
Affliction

Eggs and bacon sizzled in the cast iron frying pan while Punzel nestled jars of her best jams and jellies into a red plaid cloth-lined berry basket. Today was the last Thursday in November and a very special day for Punzel and her grandfather. They'd been invited to their first Thanksgiving Day dinner and Punzel wanted to bring her best preserves, a gift for the hostess, Mrs. Johnsson, and two blackberry pies to share with the dinner guests. She could hardly wait to meet the new family that was also invited to the celebration. *It will be fun to meet a girl my age,* she thought.

Punzel wasn't the only one doing special chores this morning.

The big shed behind the little cottage was aflutter with activity. Stig's soft brown eyes were bright as he was treated to a good brushing. Pung tied the horse to a post in the center of the shed. Then he stood on a special stool Alf had made and started brushing Stig's face first, then his body and lastly his sturdy, straight legs. The patient horse tingled with pleasure as the stiff brush removed all dirt, dust and any hint of old sweat, and made his dark brown hair shine like rich chocolate. Next Pung combed Stig's golden mane and tail, removing all hay, straw, dirt and snarls. Then he cleaned the dirt from Stig's hooves with a special pick and shined them with an oily rag. Stig loved the attention.

Arne had taken Stig's harness off the carved wall pegs, polished its brass fittings, and rubbed all its leather parts, including the reins, with oil. The week before, the wagon had been given a fresh coat of red paint and now a clean blanket lay across the high seat, ready for the day's trip.

Gotta looked on, thinking the commotion was a lot of fuss about nothing. All she cared about were the oats kept in the carved oak barrel.

"There's nothing like the smell of bacon frying on a cold fall morning, is there Pung?" Arne and Pung came in from the shed brushing off a light dusting of fresh snow from their clothes.

"I sure appreciate a nice hot breakfast after a good workout grooming Stig," Pung replied as he hung up his jacket. "I want him to look his best today."

"I got my exercise, too, cleaning and polishing Stig's harness." Arne commented as he seated himself at the trestle table.

"I'm sure glad this food won't go to waste!" Punzel teased her grandfather as he took a second helping of pancakes. "I thought you might be saving space for the big meal later today."

"I'll bet you're looking forward to meeting that Norwegian girl, Gunilla Ericksssen, eh, Punzel?" Arne teased right back. "You seem a bit distracted this morning."

"You always are able to read my mind, Farfar," laughed Punzel. "I don't know how you do it!"

"This time it wasn't difficult." Her grandfather pointed to her attire. "Your pinafore is on inside out."

"Oh, so it is." Punzel laughed after looking down at her apron. "Yes, I AM excited! The last time we had a real party was on my birthday almost two months ago. What fun we're going to have with the Johnsson's and the new neighbors. You must be looking forward to their stories of Norway. It seems like we have lived here so long that we can be considered old timers."

"Ja, I'm feeling more and more like an old timer." Arne rubbed his upper arms and elbows. "I haven't chopped so much wood in years. Your farbror spoiled me at Nordvik. My muscles are a little more achy these days."

"That's not the kind of old timer I mean, Farfar! But if you have aches, Mrs. Johnsson's cooking is a sure cure for them."

Pung listened happily to grandfather and granddaughter banter back and forth. It had been a while since either of them had been very happy. The threat of the lumbermen weighed heavily on every-one's mind. *Today they'll have a rest from the worry*, he thought. He was looking forward to dinner with his own friends, the woodland elves.

Outside, the heavy snow clouds made way for the sun as Arne hitched Stig to the wagon and Gotta gulped down her Thanksgiving Day treat of extra grain. She was glad to remain home and not have all of the exercise Stig seemed to crave. Being very particular about noises, Gotta noticed the wagon's seat springs were silent as Punzel and Arne boarded. *A good improvement! Alf didn't seem to bother about those squeaky springs. Guess he was too busy carving,* she concluded like everyone else.

The short trip to the Johnsson's farm was fairly smooth as the warm sun softened the ruts in the road. It gave the berry pies a much easier ride, too. *So far, so good,* thought Punzel, her eyes sparkled in anticipation.

They arrived at the same time as the Erickssens. The new neighbors were introduced to Arne and Punzel. Mr. Erickssen soon won Arne's favor by complimenting him on the beautiful horse and the well-kept wagon. Mrs. Johnsson graciously accepted Punzel's preserve basket. As Punzel started up the porch steps, she was greeted by a playful, hungry dog, who jumped toward the luscious smelling pies and startled her. One pie bounced out of Punzel's hands.

"Oh no! My pies!" Punzel cried out as she desperately tried to balance the remaining one. Luckily, the bouncing pie flew sideways and a quick-thinking Gunilla reached out and caught the runaway pie in flight!

"Don't worry, Punzel." Gunilla smiled when she placed the pie safely on the kitchen table. "This pie is in perfect shape and will taste just as good as your other one." Punzel knew then that Gunilla would become a good friend.

Dinner was delicious. The new arrivals to America had never known turkey or sweet potatoes. They liked the turkey stuffing, which reminded them of a favorite dessert, bread pudding, and they enjoyed the flavor of the cranberries, which they found similar to lingonberries. Punzel and Arne liked the idea of a national harvest day where people gave thanks for the plentiful foods grown during the year. Punzel was certainly thankful for the wonderful crops of raspberries, blueberries, gooseberries, and blackberries she had gathered to make her preserves that enabled her to purchase the secret birthday presents for her grandfather.

She was also thankful for her new friend. *We certainly are different,* she thought. Gunilla was not quite as tall as Punzel and had such amazing orange-red colored hair and a face full of freckles. Her younger sister, Liv, was petite with short curly brown hair and an impish smile.

The eventful day ended with a promise from the Nordströms to visit the Erickssens during the Christmas holiday. Punzel asked Mrs. Erickssen and Mrs. Johnsson if they would bring their families to Alf's cottage, (she still thought of it as Alf's) as a surprise for Arne's birthday. Punzel told them not to bring a present because their visit would be the best present for Arne. They heartily accepted Punzel's invitation and Gunilla told Punzel, "This will give us another chance to see each other and something for my sister Liv and me to look forward to before Christmas. I have enjoyed meeting you, Punzel, and l can hardly wait to see the beautiful heart-shaped pond."

•   •   •   •   •

Daylight shortened in the Tidendal Valley as fall dissolved into winter. Lamps glowed for most of the day in the little red cottage beside the heart-shaped pond. Punzel and Stig enjoyed their daily rides in the forest. They noticed deer, raccoon and rabbit tracks in the new fallen snow, but rarely did they meet a creature. Once they took Pung to a meeting of the forest elves and saw Gunvald Moose on a distant hill striding toward Lodespar Mountain. "The smaller creatures will have a tough time navigating in the deep snow," Pung had explained to them. "Soon the forest will contain a maze of tunnels connecting the smaller woodlanders' homes underneath the snow. We probably won't see the field mice and voles until spring."

"We'd better remember to stay on the main trails," Punzel reminded herself and Stig. "We wouldn't want to damage any hidden pathways."

On the thirteenth of December, in the hour before dawn when all was quiet and still, an unusual sight came to the land of the Tidendal Woods. Punzel placed a crown of lit candles on her head and, singing a traditional Swedish song, *Sankta Lucia*, she approached her grandfather's bed carrying a tray of Lucia Kattar buns, sweet rolls flavored with saffron and shaped like a cat's tail, and a steaming pot of coffee. Arne, awakened by her singing, enjoyed being served breakfast in bed.

"Punzel, you are wonderful to do this for me. For a moment, I thought I was back in Sweden."

"The Swedish Christmas season would not be properly started without a 'Lucia,' Farfar. It is right that we bring our customs to this beautiful land. I love the meaning of this special moment of peace when I see the candlelight glowing on this darkest of mornings. This is our Thanksgiving and I am truly grateful to be here with you."

Mid-afternoon brought a surprise for Punzel. Pung bounded into the cottage and handed her a package carefully wrapped in dried leaves secured with vines. "Gerda stopped by and said to give you this from the trolls at Lodespar Mountain."

"Whatever could it be?" Punzel wondered. She gently unfolded the leaves and found, nested in the center, a delicate heart-shaped silver pin with a horse in the middle. "This tiny horse is the image of Stig!" She passed the pin to her grandfather and Pung. "Look, the workmanship is perfect!"

"They are skilled craftsmen." Arne agreed, touching the little pin in admiration.

"This pin is a 'thank you' because you and Stig rescued those young trolls," Pung explained.

"I will always wear it," said Punzel. "The pin represents special friendships, not only between the trolls and us, but between Sig and me. Speaking of trolls. We haven't heard much from under the bridge. I wonder how Drekel is fairing in this cold weather."

"Oh, Drekel is doing just fine, I'm sure," Pung snorted.

"That troll is a survivor. He's too ornery to get cold."

•　　•　　•　　•　　•

Drekel had been keeping himself very warm indeed, but in a way no one would have guessed. (Practicing magic creates a lot of heat. Just ask the daisies and violets in his hair) For two full moons he grunted, babbled, vibrated, twisted, flapped and fluttered his arms and exercised his memory in an attempt to come up with some useful spells that would enable him to get the lumbermen to confess to their wrongdoing. He was definitely a troll on a mission. Gradually he felt his magical powers returning. But now he had trouble deciding the best approach to take in making the lumbermen confess. In fact, how could he approach them? They couldn't see a troll. What image could his powers conjure up? He grunted, groaned, strained, and contorted his body into very weird shapes.

"My nose is too long," he grumbled. "My hair needs clipping! These flowers have to vanish! And so does this tail!"

Then one moonlit evening, Drekel shouted, "Practice, practice makes perfect!" He stared with triumph at his reflection in the pond's clear ice. The image looking back at him was a lumberman, much like the lumbermen he has seen in the woods! *There*, he thought with great satisfaction, *what a handsome figure of a man I am, and not a tail nor a long nose to be seen! Now for the trick that is going to make them confess. Do I use sneezes, wheezes, hiccups, stickups, twitches, or itches? What an assortment of spells I have perfected! My hard work has finally paid off and soon I shall reclaim MY trees, and they will be MINE, all MINE!*

At the time Gerda delivered Dangor's present to Punzel, Drekel happened to be awake. *What a stroke of good luck,* Drekel thought as he saw the gyrfalcon arrive. He quickly transformed himself into a lumberman and approached Gerda as she was leaving.

"Excuse me, fair flier. I seem to have lost my friends. I'm wondering if you might have seen two lumbermen working near this land."

"Why, yes," replied Gerda. "I did notice two men cutting trees about three walking miles to the south."

"Thank you for your information." Drekel turned and headed south. *Hee, hee. Gerda didn't recognize me! If I can fool Gerda, I'll fool those lumbermen. No one knows I'm a troll! I have my magical powers back! My magic is back! My power is back!* He actually danced a jig in his glee.

Three miles is a long walk, but Drekel was determined and strode like the tallest of men. The problem was the exact location of the lumbermen once he reached their woods. A troll's long distance vision is not good and its hearing is not sharp. There was nothing in Drekel's magic that could change those facts. Despite his looks, he was still a troll.

When Drekel reached his destination he spent a frustrating day wandering the forest hoping to catch sight of the lumbermen or hear the sound of an ax or saw. Finally he spied the lumbermen at the edge of a clear-cut. Astonished at the amount of trees that had been felled, he gasped, "This will not happen to MY forest!" Anger welled up in him. Then he remembered he was supposed to be a lumberman. He collected his thoughts and ambled over to the tree cutters.

"Howdy! How's the work going?"

"That's our business," came the curt reply.

"I'm just trying to be friendly," Drekel countered.

"We're not interested in friendly. We're here to get our job done and leave." The lumberman gave him a threatening look.

Drekel thought to himself, *these men have worse dispositions than mountain trolls. It will be a pleasure to teach them a lesson in politeness as well.* Drekel made a well-practiced motion with his hands, ending with a goodbye wave. "Hope the rest of the day goes well for you." He winked at the two lumbermen, chuckled a small chuckle, turned and walked away.

The lumbermen stared at the retreating Drekel. "Glad to see the last of that odd character. Let's get back to work and finish this job." Each man grabbed an end of a cross-cut saw and placed it so that it would cut into the trunk of a huge oak tree. First one pulled the saw his way then it was the other's turn to pull. Each pull sent sawdust spraying. Then, sooner than one can sneeze three times, the lumbermen began to itch—here an itch, there an itch, then a scratch here, and a scratch there. Pretty soon, they were so busy scratching their itches that they were no longer able to work. They moaned and groaned. "What's happening? There must be something in that tree that doesn't agree with us. Let's try another tree."

They tried tree after tree, but the itching only got worse.

Soon they were red-faced and welts had started to form on their noses and cheeks. "We've got to get out of here, boss," said the one to the other. They were in such a hurry to leave that they didn't stop to pick up their tools. In their haste, they didn't notice the "odd character" lumberman until they practically bumped into him.

"Well, fancy running into the two of you so soon and in such a hurry! exclaimed Drekel. "What seems to be the problem?"

"I told you back there that what we do is none of your business," said the boss lumberman.

"Looks to me like you have some sort of predicament, charging through the woods like a bear was after you. You didn't even bother to take your tools," observed Drekel with a sly smile. "Must be a mighty important date."

"Get rid of that guy, boss," said the lumberman. "We don't need his kind around."

"Just a minute!" The lumber boss glared at Drekel. "You seem mighty smug. Do you know something about our rashes? We got these itches just after you left us back there."

"All I know about itches is that they come to people who tell lies and try to cheat other people." Drekel WAS feeling very smug. "Now, if you fit that description, then, I say you have a problem. Looks to me like you fit that description."

The lumbermen looked at each other. "Naw, we don't cheat people," said one lumberman. "Right boss?"

"That's right!" answered the boss lumberman. He looked at Drekel and then glanced away. "Say, what would happen if we did just a little deed that maybe wasn't totally proper, but we weren't hurting anybody by doing it?"

"I'd say that judging by your condition, that little deed was hurting a lot of somebodies," replied Drekel.

"Do you know of a remedy for this, uh, condition?" The boss lumberman was scratching his legs and had a hard time standing still.

"I sure do. Seems there's a hearing scheduled for December 20th at the meeting house in New Hope. I feel confident that showing up to tell the judge about your 'little deed' might be a sure cure for your ailment."

"Come on, boss," begged the other lumberman. "This guy is speaking gibberish. I'm going back to the boarding house. There's only one way to get rid of these itches and that's with a bath."

"Okay, okay, maybe you're right. But I still think this whole thing is mighty peculiar." The boss gave Drekel one last look and hurried after the other lumberman.

Chapter 14
Justice

The meeting house was packed with townspeople and local farmers. News of the controversy over the ownership of the magnificent trees in the Tidendal Woods had spread. Everyone wanted to see justice done.

Drekel huddled behind an empty wagon while spectators crowded into the small meeting house in the village of New Hope. Then, as the judge entered the building, no one noticed a scruffy lumberman squeeze into a standing room only space at the back of the room.

The judge seated himself behind a scarred and ink-stained desk at the front of the room. Despite the modest setting of the courtroom, the judge, dressed in a formal black robe, looked every bit the man in charge. Banging his gavel, he brought the hearing to order.

Then all eyes turned toward the lumber boss's attorney as he stood and addressed the judge. "Your honor, my client would respectfully request permission to make a statement before this hearing proceeds any further. His statement will expedite these proceedings."

The judge was surprised but replied, "Very well, if Mr. Lundquist has no objection."

"I have no objection, your honor," stated Mr. Lundquist.

"As there is no objection, your client may make his statement," the judge announced.

"Proceed," the judge said, nodding to the the lumber boss.

As the lumber boss rose from his chair it was obvious to all that he was in great discomfort. His face and hands were beet red and covered with open, runny sores and grotesque purple bumps. His scab-covered hands trembled as he tried to keep from scratching his itching arms. Lightweight loose-fitting clothing draped his blistered body and open-toed slippers cushioned his swollen feet. The heat in the stuffy crowded room only added to his discomfort. The strangeness of the lumber boss's appearance startled the room's occupants and started them buzzing with questions and comments.

"Why are his face and hands so red and lumpy?"

"Why is he wearing summer clothing in the cold of winter?"

"He looks like he just got out of bed."

"Quiet!" demanded the judge, banging his gavel for order.

The lumber boss was oblivious to everything but his itchy oozing misery. Several cool baths had done nothing to relieve the itching. On the contrary, the baths had spread the festering ooze from the boil-like sores until there was nary a spot on his body that wasn't host to his affliction. He was finally ready to believe that his only chance for recovery lay in the far-fetched hope that the odd lumberman from the forest had a remedy for this blight, but only if he, Rudy Smidgens, confessed. Rudy worked up his courage and tried to clear his throat.

A low raspy voice came out as he told the judge, "I forged Alf Nordström's signature on the tree-cutting agreement between us."

A gasp rose from the spectators. "Did he say what I thought he said?" Pandemonium raged as each questioned the other.

Again, the judge banged his gavel. "I want order. Any more outbursts and you shall all be removed from the room!"

Pung stood, scrunched between Arne's and Punzel's seats, invisible to all but his two companions. He looked around the room while everyone's attention was on the defendant repeating his statement of guilt. A solitary figure leaning against the back wall caught Pung's attention because this was the only face in the room radiating a joyful, knowing expression rather than a look of surprise. Pung studied the man's face and clothing. *They belong to someone who looks like a lumberman*, he noticed. *But there's something about him that doesn't fit his character.*

Pung's thoughts were diverted back to the judge who was admonishing the lumber boss for his deceit.

"You have harmed the good reputation of honorable lumbermen by forging Mr. Nordström's signature, but since you've come forward and confessed on your own initiative, I'll be lenient and not recommend a jail sentence. However, forgery is a serious crime and should not go unpunished. Therefore, I can't allow you, Rudy Smidgens, or your partner, who I believe was your accomplice, to remain in the lumbering business. Furthermore, neither of you will be welcome in this territory for ten years. I hope you'll learn a lesson from this and not become involved in any more mischief. Judging by your appearance, you seem to be suffering from some other disagreeable problem. One never profits by trying to cheat others and much harm can be done to innocent people. Therefore, I also expect you to give a formal apology to Alf Nordström's relatives here and now."

"Anything you say Judge, your honor." Then the lumber boss, stuttering through cracked parched lips, addressed Arne and Punzel. "I am truly sorry for causing you trouble and making you upset. . . I know what it's like to be miserable." He moved his right hand in a soothing manner over his chest. "Please accept my apology."

"Your apology is accepted," Arne replied. "It does appear that you've had enough punishment for a while."

Satisfied, the judge turned to Rudy's attorney. "See to it that your client abides by my decisions. I want his lumber business terminated and him and his friend out of this territory within twenty-four hours."

"Yes, your Honor," came the attorney's reply.

"This hearing is over! Court is dismissed," announced the judge, and down went the gavel for the last time.

Arne, Punzel and Mr. Lundquist were congratulated on the outcome as Rudy Smidgens painfully limped out of the meeting room. The onlookers stepped aside to let him pass as no one wanted to come in contact with him lest they catch his illness.

Drekel melted into the retreating crowd, satisfied that his spell had brought the desired results. *MY trees are safe, My peace is preserved.* (It was an elated troll who trudged home whistling an old troll tune.)

The lumber boss and his companion would suffer a few more days with their itches. A small, red, neck rash would remain on each lumberman as a reminder that cheating never pays, especially when a determined troll is around.

•   •   •   •   •

"Farfar, I feel like dancing!" Punzel twirled over the smooth cottage floor. Her flaxen braids stood straight out from her head while her skirt billowed and whirled like a spinning top. Arne and Pung clapped their hands in rhythm as they watched the light-footed, energetic young woman dance.

"That's how she stays slim," her two rotund companions agreed.

Punzel finally wound down and plopped on the stool asking, "I wonder what made that lumber boss confess? I still can't believe it happened."

"I can't quite believe it myself," Arne replied. "Rudy Smidgens sure was an unscrupulous character. My bror wasn't able to understand a person like that. I guess that's what did old Alf in. Mr. Smidgens had better be careful. He didn't look particularly healthy. Those rashes sure looked like something didn't agree with him. Ha, ha, wouldn't it be funny if he suddenly developed a sensitivity to sawdust. Not much lumbering can be done when you suffer around wood. Maybe all the discomfort caused his change of heart."

Punzel's blue eyes sparkled with mirth. "Farfar, you've become a good story teller."

Sensitivities, Pung thought. *Hummm. I wonder . . . that isn't so far-fetched at all.* He thought about the odd-looking lumberman at the back of the meeting hall. The longer and harder Pung thought, the more he was convinced that there was something different about the man. *That lumberman's hair was unusually coarse and thick and odd. He didn't take his cap off indoors like the rest of the men folks. Why not? Hummm. There was something else, something yellow! Yes! That's it! There was something yellow peeking out from under his cap. It looked like a yellow pansy. At this time of year!* Pung's eyes suddenly lit up as he chuckled and jumped up and down. He felt like dancing too.

"Pung!" Punzel watched the little elf with amusement. "What are you up to? You look positively giddy. Do you know why the lumber boss confessed?"

"I have my suspicions," he replied with a mischievous wink.

110

Chapter 15
The Hero

Your brambleberry pies are almost done," Pung announced as he poked his head out the front door. "How is your snowman coming?"

Punzel had just finished putting two lumps of coal, for eyes, and a long carrot nose into the head of a very plump snowman in the front yard of the little red cottage by the heart-shaped pond. "The snowman is finished!" She wrapped Alf's old scarf around the snowman's neck and plopped a battered cap on the top of his head. "Won't the Erickssens and Johnssons be surprised to be greeted by such a good-looking man when they come to Farfar's birthday party this afternoon? Yummy! I can smell the pies from here." Punzel sniffed as she bounded up the front steps. "Thanks for watching the pies so that I could build my snowman. Do you know where our birthday boy went with Stig and the wagon?" She watched Pung open the heavy oven door.

"He hinted that it was a surprise and he wouldn't be gone long."

"Farfar's full of secrets." Punzel put the pies on the sideboard to cool.

"There are only three days left before Christmas." Pung reminder her. "I'm sure the results of his mysterious projects will be revealed then. Alf was like that too. He was always able to keep a good secret. I remember the Christmas he built my bed and then put it in the loft without my knowing about it. From then on, I slept in the cottage instead of the shed. That was one of my best presents ever!"

"Just like Farfar did for my birthday! The Nordström men are very kind and thoughtful. Far is like that also." Punzel's face became a little sad. "I really miss him, especially at this time of year. I hope he and Anna got the table cloth I sent for Christmas. I stitched the year 1907 on one corner as a remembrance of their first married Christmas together. I've worked very hard on my embroidery stitches. He will see how much my sewing has improved since I've been making my own clothes. When I was younger a dressmaker made my clothes. Pung, I've really grown up at lot since we arrived here. Imagine that! I'm even giving my own dinner party."

Pung had been sitting on the kitchen counter looking out the window while they talked. "Punzel, do you mind if I go out for a little walk?" he asked, while he jumped down from his seat. You and Arne will be busy entertaining your guests and I'll just be in the way."

"You're never in the way, Pung," said Punzel, "but if you would really like to go for a walk, that would be fine. I'll save you and Drekel some pie."

Punzel set the trestle table with eight red checkered place mats and eight red napkins using Alf's carved napkin rings. Then she encircled Alf's four-armed red wooden candleholder with small pine branches for the table's centerpiece. She sniffed the sweet smell of the brambleberry pies mixed with the aroma of hot, fresh ground coffee. *How nice it is to live in this wonderful place*, she thought as she admired the deep green pine boughs with bright red bows framing the cottage windows and doors. The little room sparkled with holiday spirit as the guests arrived.

"What fun to be greeted by your snowman!" Mrs. Erickssen and Mrs. Johnsson told Punzel as they entered the warm little cottage, each carrying a basket of food.

"Oh, my goodness," exclaimed Punzel. "You didn't have to bring all of that food. The pickled cucumbers, carrots and beans look wonderful. I didn't have time to preserve any of those. Tack så mycket!"

"Var så god! These are just a few little dishes we thought you might enjoy over the holidays," they explained. "Your cottage is very cozy and festive." Mrs. Erickssen admired the cheerful table settings and decorations. "I hope our farm house will look as nice when we're more settled."

"It sure smells good!" chimed in Liv, the ever-hungry twelve year old.

"Where is Arne?" Farmer Johnsson came in the door after caring for his horse. "I see that his horse and wagon are not in the shed."

112

Mr. Erickssen removed his heavy coat as he joined the party a few minutes later, "Mr. Nordström just pulled into the backyard."

Punzel had just hung up the guests' coats and hats when the back door swung open and Arne stood in the entrance. "Well, what have we here? I leave for a little while and come back to find the cottage full of neighbors. What's the occasion?"

"Happy birthday!" everyone shouted.

"This is a pleasant surprise!" Arne smiled. "It's nice to see the Erickssens again." He nodded at Mrs. Erickssen and shook hands with Mr. Erickssen, and greeted the Johnssons.

"Do you want to see the pond while we still have plenty of daylight?" Punzel asked Gunilla and Liv.

"Yes," they both eagerly replied. Punzel, remembering her manners, served the adults coffee first. "I promised I would show the heart-shaped pond to Gunilla and Liv," she explained as the girls put on their overcoats.

"Go, young ones," said her grandfather. "I'll show the Erickssens Alf's carvings while you're gone."

The mirrored surface of the pond reflected the low-slung puffy winter clouds, evoking a picture from the tales of "The Snow Queen." Tiny balls of fluffy snow that looked like pussy willow buds clung to the branches of the brambleberry bushes. "Your pond is a fairy tale setting," described Liv, who was a fan of Hans Christian Andersen.

"Yes," agreed Gunilla. "It really does have a mystical quality. Look, there's an otter playing at the far end. How delightful. May we go on the bridge to see him better?"

"Yes . . . of course," Punzel, answered with a little trepidation. "But we must be very quiet," she warned the enthusiastic Liv. To herself Punzel thought, *I hope Drekel is sleeping very soundly.*

It was hard to be very quiet as the crisp snow crunched and squeaked under their boots. However, no one below was disturbed, and Punzel breathed a sigh of relief as they left the bridge and returned to the cottage. The guests were admiring the carvings on Alf's closet bed as Punzel, Gunilla and Liv hurried to take off their outer clothing and snuggle up to the warmth of the fireplace.

Dinner was light-hearted with laughter and good conversation. Just as everyone declared they couldn't eat another bite, Punzel served the sugar-crusted brambleberry pies. Their mouth-watering fragrance tantalized everyone into trying "just a small piece."

113

"What kind of fruit is this?" asked Mrs. Erickssen.

"It's called brambleberry." Punzel told her that Alf mentioned the berries in his journal. "I thought the berries might make good pie filling so I preserved them for Farfar's birthday. I've only found them growing by the pond's bridge so they might be quite rare."

"They do make delicious pies, Punzel," said Mrs. Johnsson. "You are a fine cook."

Punzel blushed with pleasure. "Tack. That is quite a compliment coming from you."

Her grandfather beamed with pleasure. "You are a wonderful hostess, Punzel. You have made this a very special birthday."

After dinner Punzel showed Gunilla and Liv the loft. While the Ericksen girls admired Punzel's bed, the doll-sized furniture by the chimney caught Liv's interest. "What cute furniture," she exclaimed. "Where is your doll?"

"My dolls are back in Sweden." Punzel answered. "Alf made this furniture a long time ago."

"Would you like one of my dolls to live here?" Liv picked up the little log chair, her dark curls bounced across her face.

Punzel brushed the younger girl's hair back with her hand and thanked her for the offer. Then she replied without further explanation, "The furniture does get some use."

Farmer Johnsson announced that he must get back to his farm and feed their sheep. The Erickssens said that they too had chores to do. The afternoon had passed all too quickly for everyone. They renewed their agreement to get together after Christmas and then the Nordströms' neighbors departed.

While Punzel and her grandfather waved good bye, Punzel's thoughts returned to a question she had asked Pung earlier. "Farfar where did you go this morning?"

"Ah, my little one," Arne teased, "you are so curious. But since you fixed such a wonderful birthday dinner, you deserve to know. Come with me to the shed."

Arne lit the lantern hanging by the back door and into the cold, crisp air they walked side by side, following the moving circle of light toward the shed door. When Arne opened the door, the light stretched across the darkness. "What are you two doing out here at this time of night?" Gotta questioned as she stepped into the light.

"I promised Punzel she could see what I was doing with the wagon this afternoon," Arne replied.

"Are you going to take it away from us?" Gotta asked.

"Take what away from you?" Punzel was perplexed.

"Look at what's on the back of the wagon," Stig directed her. The lantern light skipped over patches of straw on the earthen floor and up the wagon's sideboards. Punzel watched the light come to rest on a beautifully shaped, six-foot-tall fir tree.

"Our Christmas tree! You got our Christmas tree, Farfar," Punzel cried with delight.

"Do you like it?" Pung, covered with snow, opened the shed door.

"There you are. You look like you were in a snowball fight. Must have been an eventful walk." Punzel surveyed the little elf. "Yes, I think the tree is beautiful!

Arne lifted the tree off the wagon and stood it on the dirt floor in front of Punzel. "I was going to ask you to come with me this morning, but then I noticed how busy you were." He winked at this remark. "I saw this tree yesterday so I decided to dig it up and bring it back as a surprise. You don't mind do you?"

"Nej, Farfar. I've had so much on my mind that I haven't thought about a Christmas tree. You dug it up?"

"Ja. I didn't have the heart to destroy the tree so I covered its roots with earth and burlap feed sacks. Luckily the snow kept the ground soft so it was easy to dig. We'll plant it in the spring where your snowman stands," he declared.

"After you use it in the cottage can you bring it back to the shed until you plant it?" requested Gotta and Stig.

"Ja, of course, my animal friends," Arne laughed. "I will bring it back here after Christmas."

"Pung," Punzel reminded the elf, "don't forget that I saved you and Drekel each a piece of pie. We did miss you at the party."

She gave the elf a rather quizzical look as Pung ran to deliver a piece of pie to Drekel.

After Arne and Punzel said good night to the animals, Punzel told her grandfather she had a surprise for him, too. "Another surprise? You have given me enough surprises already, my dear."

"Close your eyes," she told him as they entered the cottage. Then she led Arne over to his bed and opened the bed's doors. "Now you can open your eyes." There on the coverlet lay a navy blue wool shirt and a package of salt licorice.

"Punzel, you are the dearest barnbarn." Arne gave her a big hug. "How did you manage to buy this shirt and my favorite candy? I know you didn't have much money."

"I sold my jams and jellies at Mr. Nelson's store." Punzel admitted with pride. "Actually Pung deserves part of the credit because he took care of the gardens while I gathered the berries. Mr. Nelson said that he will buy as many preserves as I can make. I have a way to earn money, Farfar."

"What a clever young lady you are!" The proud grandfather hugged his granddaughter again. "I will thank Pung when he comes in. When we were in the shed, I meant to ask Pung why he wasn't at my party, but he left too soon."

"He told me he was going for a walk just before our guests arrived," Punzel explained. "There was a strange gleam in his eye and then he made some excuse about being in our way, which we all know isn't true. I'll bet he was up to something and he didn't want to tell me what it was."

•   •   •   •   •

Pung had been up to something. Before Arne's party, he had spied Drekel heading for the woods. *A walk in the woods during daylight! I wonder where that troll is going. This is my chance to catch up with that fellow.* After he gave Punzel that rather lame excuse to leave, he pulled his long red cap over his ears, grabbed his jacket, donned his boots and scooted out the back door before Punzel could question him further.

Drekel didn't travel fast, but Pung's short legs against the drifting snow made him even slower. It took him quite a while to catch up.

"Hi," Pung spoke, a little out of breath.

"Hi, yourself," Drekel replied, casting a weary eye in Pung's direction.

"That sure was a nice bit of work getting that lumber boss to confess to signing Alf's name to that tree contract," Pung blurted out, hoping to catch the troll unaware.

"What are you talking about?" retorted the indignant troll.

"I thought you were very clever to think of a way to get that lumber man to confess." Pung decided flattery was a good approach. "I'm delighted to find that you have changed your outlook."

"Clever! That I am, but my so-called outlook is no concern of

116

yours. By the way, what makes you think I could do anything to make him confess?"

"Your magical powers are back! You've been practicing," declared the smug elf.

"What I have been doing is none of your business." Drekel glared down at the little red hat.

"Well, I know that the success of a Lodespar troll's magic depends on the troll having an honorable attitude," Pung glared back at the troll.

"You're babbling, babbling, babbling! You elves know nothing about troll magic!" Drekel asserted.

"You can't fool me." Pung ignored the insult. "Like it or not, you championed the saving of those ancient trees for us all—the animals, the forest and the Nordströms."

"That's absurd!" quipped the troll.

"Then how do you explain the return of your magical powers?" demanded Pung.

"Okay. Practice, pure and simple!" retorted Drekel.

"Don't be silly!" Pung was really enjoying this. "That's not all! Your troll magic would not have returned without you considering the feelings of others. Remember, you've tried your magical skills for years and found them to be steadily declining. No amount of practice brought them back before," Pung reasoned.

"How do you know it was my magic that gave the lumbermen their rashes?" Drekel unwittingly said.

"Rashes! Ah, ha!" (Pung knew that he was right and continued his quest.) "I saw you standing at the back of the meeting hall disguised as a lumberman."

"How did you know that was me?" Drekel asked.

"I saw one of your yellow pansies peeking out from under your cap." Pung was sure he had the troll now.

"DRAT THOSE FLOWERS! THEY NEVER LEAVE ME ALONE," roared the exasperated troll. "So maybe magic isn't an exact science. Now I suppose you're going to tell the whole world that Drekel has gone soft! Well, I'm telling you that I did it for ME, for MY woods! GOT THAT?"

"Oh, yes." said the elf. "Your secret is safe with me, but I don't think it will be long before others figure it out. By the way, Punzel is saving you a piece of brambleberry pie which I will bring to the bridge when I get back home."

Drekel licked his lips but concealed his pleasure by stating, "That girl stole my berries last summer." However, these words didn't cut with their usual sharpness.

Pung kicked the fluffy snow with one up-turned boot. "I've missed Arne's birthday party and Punzel will be wondering why my walk took so long. I'd better get going. Be seeing you," he called back to Drekel as he leaped over real and imaginary clumps of snow. *Magical rashes! What will that troll think of next?* He stopped every so often to scoop up a handful of snow, throw it into the air and run under the snow as it fell down. He was a very happy elf.

Drekel watched the elf, a scowl on his craggy troll face. *My reputation is going downhill fast as a rolling snowball.* Whatever had brought him to the woods in daylight had left his mind. He turned and clomped back to his bridge, hoping that Pung would hurry with that piece of pie.

Chapter 16
Magic

Punzel awoke hours before dawn and listened to the dark quiet of the resting winter forest. She shoved aside her cozy colorful quilt, stretched, braided her hair and washed, using the large bowl and pitcher by her bedside. Then she put on the special folk dress she had worn at her father's wedding, adding two extra petticoats and a sweater for warmth. *I hardly recognize me as the same girl who wore this dress last summer,* she thought as she looked at herself in the small oval mirror on the loft wall.

Four candles softly glowed on the trestle table and the logs in the fireplace crackled and sparked amidst the fragrant aroma of steaming coffee from a copper pot on the hearth. Punzel joined her grandfather for coffee and a breakfast roll.

"God Jul," she greeted him with a special smile, for this was the day of peace and joy. "The coffee smells especially good this morning."

"That's because you know we won't be eating breakfast until our church's Jul-otta service is over," her grandfather suggested with a knowing smile.

Punzel hugged him. "I want you to know how much I love and appreciate you."

"You are my little kära, barnbarn!" He gently returned the affection. "Have you had enough to eat? We need to be on our way."

Pung brought a fresh blast of winter air with him as he entered the back door and announced that Stig was groomed and feeling his oats, ready for the early morning race to the little white church on the hill.

The sleigh bells jingled to the rhythmic beat of Stig's hoofs as they struck the crisp crunchy snow. *Farfar has been very busy*, Punzel reflected as she enjoyed the smooth glide of the sleigh's runners. Arne had discovered the little sleigh under discarded blankets and tools in a corner of the large shed. He had renewed the sleigh with a fresh coat of black paint and added red and yellow decorative flowers to the sides. Punzel felt the warmth from her new long red wool hooded coat that shielded her from the cold brisk winter morning air. Arne had also found time to make iron hooks and plant holders that he exchanged at Mr. Nelson's general store for Punzel's new coat.

As their sleigh emerged from the forest, they beheld a scene that could have been from another folk tale. They saw the parishioners' sleighs and wagons converging at the road near the bottom of a hill. Their swinging lanterns cast radiant rings of light against the early morning darkness. More illumination came from miniature glowing caves of candlelight that lined each side of the ribbon-like road as it wound its way to the hill's crown where the church stood like a miniature white castle. A single candle glowed in each of its tall, narrow windows.

"There they are!" Arne's frosty voice broke the spell. Ahead was the Johnssons' sleigh, its lantern already declaring victory. Then they spotted the Erickssens' wagon on a side road coming on fast. This was going to be a close race! Farmer Johnsson's sleigh was pulled by two horses. The large wooden wheels on the Erickssen wagon were no match for runners on snow. Unbelievably, the Erickssen wagon arrived first at the winding church road and Mr. Erickssen became the winner. The church road was too narrow for another sleigh or wagon to pass.

"Ding. Dong. Ding. Dong. Ding. Dong." The church bells rang loudly through the clear morning air greeting the winner and all his followers.

"It is good that Mr. Erickssen, the newest member of the community, wins the race and gets his breakfast first. We had coffee and rolls, so we are not so hungry for frukost. Eh, Punzel?"

"I'll be good and hungry after the church service, Farfar. I hope everyone will like my lingonberry preserves. I brought a few jars to share and maybe it will be good for sales next year when we have more berries."

"You have a good business head, Punzel," Arne whispered with pride and a hidden chuckle.

The Christmas morning service was solemn and beautiful, bestowing hope on all of those early settlers who worked so hard to improve their land and the course of their lives.

The community breakfast was festive. Two long tables overflowed with homemade foods—crisp hard breads and soft, sweet, braided carda-mon bread, yellow and white cheese with or without holes, ham, herring, dilled pickles and pickled beets. There were jams, jellies, marmalades and precious fresh apples and pears that had been carefully stored in root cellars for this special occasion. Coffee was served from large pots at the end of each table. Punzel thought these serving tables rivaled any smörgåsbord in Sweden. Punzel and Arne ate with the Johnssons, Erickssens and the Karlssons, a family who lived in New Hope.

After breakfast, the adults relaxed and exchanged news while the younger ones played tag and musical chairs to work off pent-up energies. Punzel watched the children with interest, but every once in a while she would catch Gus Larsson watching her. Then she would feel the familiar color rise in her cheeks. *Goodness, I don't want him to think I'm flirting,* she scolded herself. Eventually Gus sat down next to Punzel and asked Arne if they had experienced a nice Julafton. Arne replied that their Christmas Eve had been very pleasant indeed and thanked Gus for the small candles he had given them for their Christmas tree.

Punzel found this opportunity to again tell Gus how much she liked her birthday gift. "Your can-dles smell just like fresh honey. They are a comfort in the dark mornings and winter evenings."

"I'm glad you are still enjoying them," Gus told her. "By the way, do you like to ice skate?"

"I love to ice skate, but I didn't bring my skates as our visit was only to last the three months of warm weather."

"My cousin Maja has a pair that you could borrow." Gus was gaining courage. "Would it be too bold of me to ask if you would go skating with me?"

"Why, I think that would be fun, Gus." Punzel felt another flush to her cheeks. "We could skate on our pond. The wind has kept it clear as glass. We just have to stay away from the far end as the otter plays there and has made a few holes in the ice."

Gus then asked Arne for permission to visit Punzel. Arne gave his permission. With obvious pleasure, Gus turned back to Punzel, "I will stop by with the skates in a couple of days."

Punzel watched Gus walk back to his parents table. Then she thought about Gus's candles on their special living Christmas tree. Arne had placed the tree in the center of the little cottage on Christmas Eve afternoon and together they had fastened the candles to the tree with metal candleholders that he had bent out of strong wire. The upper end of each wire wrapped around the candle and hooked over the tree branch. The other end of the wire speared into a small apple which balanced the candle above, holding it upright. They had carefully lit the three dozen small candles, keeping a bucket of water handy in case of mishaps. The exquisite fir tree had gleamed like a princess aglow with sparkling jewels. The magic of candlelight had permeated the cottage with its gracious radiance.

As the sun rose over the treetops, the families and friends of the little white church on the hill wished each other a last "God Jul" and "Merry Christmas." At a slower pace this time, the sleighs and wagons turned toward home. "This has been a glorious Jul," Punzel said to her grandfather as their sleigh bells echoed her happy thoughts. She wrapped her new coat closer and smiled as she remembered the look on her grandfather's face when he saw the hand knit red, blue and white sweater with a snowflake pattern. Pung also had a surprised, pleased look on his face when she gave him the red scarf and mittens that matched his hat. She was glad they liked her presents. Pung said he couldn't wait to show them off to his woodland friends. *He's becoming more social with the forest elves,* Punzel thought, *just like me. It's good to have friends.*

"What a nice homecoming." Punzel said to Arne as they arrived to see a flurry of sparrows, starlings and yellow chickadees feeding from the sheaves of grain that Pung had tied to a stick and placed by the snowman in their front yard.

Stig and Gotta also got special treatment. They looked forward to that extra scoop of oats from Alf's carved wooden barrel.

Punzel thought she would spend Christmas Day afternoon sitting by the fireplace reading one of those beckoning books from the tall bookcase. Arne had another idea. He told her to change into play clothes and meet him by the pond in a few minutes. Then he disappeared out the back door.

Punzel hurried as fast as she could, fairly tripping over her boots in haste. Braids flying, she bounded across the crusty snow toward the pond. Arne was waiting for her, standing beside a sled with a high seat and two ski-like long metal runners and a hand bar. "Jump on," he invited, pointing toward the seat.

"Oh, Farfar, what fun," she cried with delight. "Where did you ever find a kick sled?"

"I didn't find it, I made it." Punzel sat down on the seat. Arne stood behind the sled, placed one boot on a long back runner, and kicked forward from the ice with his other boot, then placed it on the parallel runner. Off they sailed, gliding on the narrow metal runners over the smooth hard ice. Kick, slide, kick, slide. Back and forth across and around the frozen heart-shaped pond. They took turns pushing each other, laughing and shouting like two small children. Torv and Lucia did not appear, but Bertil stopped his sliding to watch as the twosome skidded around the little island, coming dangerously close to one of Bertil's ice holes. Drekel finally poked his head out from under the icicle-laden bridge and bumped his head into a few ice spears that shattered onto the pond's frozen surface. "God Jul," Punzel and Arne called to him as they swirled past.

"Good what?" he yelled back.

"Merry Christmas, Drekel," came the reply.

"Whatever," he said and disappeared behind the ice-laden vines.

"Would you believe that?" Punzel declared, astonishment on her face. "Christmas must be affecting Drekel. He didn't grumble.

"Ja, there's hope for that troll." Arne thought this a perfect Christmas Day.

Just then a snowball whizzed by their heads. Plop! The next one hit Punzel on her back sending snow down her neck. She jumped off of the sled and hurried to the snow-covered shore. "Pung, you mischief maker!" The snowballs began to fly in both directions.

Glossary of Swedish Terms

av	of
Augusti	August
barnbarn	grandchild
bror	brother
far	father
farfar	grandfather on the father's side
farmor	grandmother on the father's side
Februari	February
fru	wife
fruktost	breakfast
god day	good day
God Jul	Merry Christmas
god natt	Good night
Göteborg	Sweden's second largest city situated at the mouth of the Göta River on the Swedish west coast, Punzel's and Arne's port of departure to the New World
Gud	God
ja	yes
Jul-otta	early Christmas morning church service
Januari	January
Jul	Christmas
Julafton	Christmas Eve
Juli	July
Juni	June
kära	dear
nej	no
Mariestad	a town in Sweden situated on the east coast of Lake Vänern on the Tida River, Punzel's birth place
Midsommar	a Scandinavian festival celebrating the summer solstice usually held the weekend nearest June 21
mor	mother
Nordström	northern stream, last name of Punzel and Arne, Americanized to Nordstrom
Nordvik	northern bay, name of Arne's Swedish farm
Oktober	October
smörgåsbord	a festive Scandinavian buffet table
tack	thank you
tack så mycket	thank you very much
tidskrift	a journal
tomtar	several elves
tomte	elf
Vänern Lake	largest lake in Sweden and Western Europe

125

About the Author

Judy Hauser spent the summers of her early life in a log cabin, built by her Swedish grandparents, on Walloon Lake. Those happy childhood memories enticed her to return to northern Michigan where she and her husband, Bernd, raised their sons, Kurt and Erik on 90 acres south of Traverse City. *The Legend of Punzel's Pond*, Judy's first book, reflects her love of Scandinavian folklore and its connection to nature.

The Hausers' pastoral property, reminiscent of the hills and lakes of Scandinavia, led to the building of a Swedish "stuga," or cottage, for a studio and gift shop which they named Punzel Scandinavian. The shop is dedicated to Judy's grandparents and over the past two decades has become a destination for those who like natural gourmet food and quality handcrafted gifts. A place to relax out of the century past.

For more information about Punzel Scandinavian, see www.punzelscandinavian.com on the internet.